A LOOK
BEYOND

Dreams, Nightmares, and
Visions of the Last Days

DAVID E. SIRIANO

A Look Beyond: Dreams, Nightmares, and Visions of the Last Days
Copyright 2017 by David E. Siriano

ISBN: 978-1-942056-33-1

Library of Congress Control Number: 2016955750
Printed in the U.S.A.

Dedication

To my son David of Oviedo, Florida. God has given him a great talent as a videographer dedicated to helping the homeless who need shelter. He is married to Glenda and they have five children.

To my daughter Darla of Rochester, NY. God has blessed her with an anointed ministry as a Pastor and ministers to those who need salvation and healing. She is married to Pastor Steve and they have three children.

To Sam and Jean Shearer and Wally and Joanne Lundstrom, friends that we have spent countless numbers of hours with in fellowship and friendship.

April 2017

Contents

Introduction

For years I have had this tremendous love to talk about the coming of the Lord and of the glories of heaven. I am not sure of all the reasons why I have been enthralled with the prospect of knowing about the future with God, but it is a love that will not let me go.

I received that spirit and love of heaven from God, but it was impressed on me by my earthly father as well. I knew of his desire to leave earth and be with the Lord. He was saved and converted to the protestant faith before I was born. One day I will see him and thank him.

I was called of God when I was 10 years old and knew that one day I would be a minister of the gospel. Perhaps I received that spirit from my father as well.

I became a Pastor in November of 1963, just weeks before President John Kennedy was assassinated. It was at that time that many approached me about what was going to happen to America and if this was a sign of the soon return of the Lord.

I was always interested in the End-Times as I studied it to prepare for the ministry in the Bible School that I attended, but it was within the next decade after I became a Pastor that I started on a long journey and lifetime study of the Second Coming of Christ.

With all of that in my mind, it is with pleasure that I give you my thoughts of this novel on the Book of Revelation. I only hope to help others understand this marvelous and final work of the canon of scripture that I love and enjoy.

In documenting each chapter, I had to imagine what heaven will be like and what the horror of the Great Tribulation will bring to the earth through the life of a man named Joseph. My only hope is that it will awaken a new understanding of the Book of Revelation for you. I trust that it will help you take to heart the entire Word of God as you let it be a part of your life.

Sincere appreciation to my wife Elsa May Larson Siriano for helping me with editing. She contributed to the ending plot that I feel will make a greater impact for the ministry that all of us have before the Lord returns. She also made additions to some of the story line.

A special thank you to my daughter Darla Jean Siriano Edlin, Co-Pastor of Faith Temple in Rochester, New York. She provided me with the title.

I want this labor of love to encourage you to be a witness to those who need Christ. Our generation must sound a warning of Christ's soon return just like others have done in the past in order to avoid the devastation that is to come.

Chapter One: Revelation of God

My name is Joseph. I was born in Pennsylvania and was one of five siblings born to a middle class family. I was raised by parents that taught me to believe in God. We attended church and I knew what it was like to hear the obligatory sermon each week. I always believed that I needed to put into practice what I was taught and what I learned. I wasn't perfect but I tried to live my life in obedience to God's word. I believed in what the Bible said to be as *"a wise man who built his house on the rock: and the rain descended, the floods came, and the winds blew and beat on that house; and it did not fall, for it was founded on the rock."* I wanted to be that strong in the Lord and as a married man, I wanted to teach my family to be that strong as well.

One warm and sunny summer day as I awoke, I felt that it was going to be just like any other day. I was up early and drove off to my high school teaching job and arrived on time. The ride was the usual busy highway traffic. The sky was beautiful and the weather was clear. I felt good about myself and my life. I couldn't think of anything that could be any better than the great day that God gave me to enjoy.

I loved my job and the interaction with my students and I think that they respected me and my ability as a teacher. When I

9

A Look Beyond

arrived at my school desk, I was very busy keeping my mind occupied with some of my teaching assignments. I was also thinking ahead as to what some of my projects were going to be that would keep me busy today and the rest of the week. I was living in a "dog eat dog" world and I was concentrating on how I was going to keep ahead of my reading, note preparation and grading of papers.

My thoughts were very deep into my work and I was hoping to hear a solid 'well done' from the principal and a pat on the back from my fellow teachers. I thought about my home life and my four brothers and sisters but I also was so thankful for my wife and three sons. As good as I felt, I was doing my best to live in a world that seemed to be spinning morally out of control and I was learning to deal with all the financial stress and drain that was engulfing my life.

My mind couldn't help but wander. I am a Christian and filled with the Spirit of God, so spiritual thoughts would constantly enter my thinking process. Growing up in church all of my life I continually heard the Old Testament stories about the men and women who lived for God even in troubled times. The book of the Bible I liked the most was the book of Psalms that inspired me and helped me by encouraging me when my life was overtaken in frivolous matters. Also, in my mind I was constantly reminded about the life and teachings of Jesus in the gospels and of the writings of the Apostles.

When I was a young man I continually heard about the Second Coming of Jesus Christ in church. I heard so many inspiring stories about an eternity with God and what it would be like to live in heaven forever. With so many things taking up my time, would I be ready for the coming of the Lord? We were always taught to anticipate and be ready for this event that we believed was soon to come. No one knows when it will occur so we have to be prepared in our heart.

LOVE OF GOD'S WORD

Week after week went by in my life as I continued in my daily Bible readings. I love reading God's Word and tried to commit as much of it to memory as I possibly could. I must admit that I was most fascinated with the book of Revelation and concentrated heavily on the drama and visions that it unfolded. Even though I knew about the Second Coming of Christ and sensed that Revelation had a lot to do with it, to me the book was scary and troubling because I didn't always understand what it was all about. It was very difficult to know its meaning but just like so many other people I still loved reading it because I felt it was part of God's Word. I had many conversations with family members and friends about the future events that were written in that most misunderstood book.

I was always told that it had a wide view of interpretations. Some felt that it was purely fictional while others felt that that the events recorded in it had already happened in past history. Still others said that it was highly symbolic while those who interpreted it literally felt that it was still going to be fulfilled in the future. I never could totally grasp it all but I thought that the future view was the best way to interpret it because of all of the things that were happening in the world today. I never seriously considered any of the other views to be that accurate or that important to me.

I believed in Jesus as my Savior which was a great experience for me but that wasn't enough for my curious mind. I wanted to know more and especially what evangelical preachers and evangelists called the 'rapture.' Even with all of the discourse they commanded in their speaking and with all of those who believed in the rapture, there were still some who did not believe it at all. Others debated as to when it would take place in the future. Was it before the great evil that will fall on the earth in what the Bible calls the Great Tribulation, was it during that time or was it after that time? To me, debating about the timing of the rapture didn't interest me at all. I just felt that God was going to do what He wanted to do anyway. Despite all of the difference of opinion I was enthralled by the prospect of being taken from this life to heaven and into the very presence of God to live with Him forever.

I asked myself, "How is the rapture possible?" "What would it be like?" "Who would I see, if anyone?" "Would I remember those who lived on earth when I was alive like my parents and brothers and sisters?" "I felt sure that I would I still know my wife, my three sons and my grandchildren who were so precious to me all of my married life." "I surely wanted them to remember me." I had many questions but the most important one to me was, "Would I know God as much as I believe He knew me?" I wanted to know everything I could. If there was a rapture I wanted to be in a state of consciousness to see everything that was happening.

While all of these thoughts were swirling in my mind, it seemed as if I was being prepared for something immediate and dramatic that was about to take place. My heart was beating fast and no sooner than I thought on those things that something happened that would change my life forever! I was overcome by the bright and sunny day that it was! I felt the warmth of activity and the sense of being needed. I felt a goodness that was swelling up inside of me.

TRANSLATION

All of a sudden there rose within me a rushing sensation. It was like something heavy was being lifted off of me and out of my life. It almost felt like I was being taken out of my body. I couldn't believe it but it seemed like I was leaving the earth. I thought, this is crazy! It was as if the room and everything in it was spinning as a light-headedness gripped my mind and my spirit. I had a sense of weightlessness as this new experience confronted me. A bright light seemed to encompass my body and lift my soul in great ecstasy and expectation. I have to admit I was scared. I didn't know what was going to happen to me.

It felt like the components inside my body were changing. I was being lifted out of my chair. What started out as slow-motion in my mind's eye, suddenly changed when everything began to move at a high rate of speed, faster than I could have imagined. My life on earth seemed unimportant and the things of the earth no longer meant anything to me. I was still conscious of time but time was now irrelevant.

The brilliant light that I saw was cascading and ascending all around me. I was being taken from the room. It seemed as if the walls and roof of the building were nothing as I passed through them with ease. I never experienced anything like this before. Did I take a leave of my senses? I then realized in my mind and my body that I began to leave this earth as I passed through the atmosphere and rose above it. I had this unreal sensation as I began to see flashes of light in what seemed to be galaxies, stars, and planets passing me by. Comets and black holes appeared in front of me and then all of a sudden they weren't there anymore. Quasars, the most distant and luminous objects known to man in the universe disappeared. Just that quick, millions of galaxies as well as the entire universe were gone! Did I really see all of those things or was it just my imagination? Was I dreaming? Was I living in an alternate state of consciousness? It's as if I was in another dimension.

I was leaving my present understanding of earthly reality and I was evolving in my mind and heart into a heavenly reality. Nothing could hold me back, not even my deepest thoughts of life on earth, and not even the fears and drudgery of common ideals and principles. Where were the feelings of anger, loneliness, bitterness, regret, and hatred? Where were the thoughts of all the events that happened in my life? They were all gone! I felt that I was as light as a feather. My inner struggles were no longer there.

What was happening? Had I been sick and now I was dying or was this really the rapture that came racing into my mind that I heard so much about? All I knew was that a wonderful release of peace had gripped my mind and spirit. I was conscious that others were traveling with me as I was being transported with millions of souls from all walks of life and from all around the world. I don't know how I knew it but some of those being transported had been dead while others had been alive like me during this powerful transformation.

I did have a momentary concern for my wife, three sons and their families but a powerful peace came over me and I felt at ease about them as well. I felt in my spirit that they would be alright. Somehow I knew that they were traveling with me. I just didn't see them. I was in such a heavenly state, as my mind, body and spirit raced me toward what I absolutely knew would be an encounter with God. I couldn't believe it but I was at total peace.

While I was leaving the earth I was able in some way to know that there were others who were being negatively impacted by the events that I was passing through. Even though the things of earth now seemed unimportant, I could look back just briefly and see the heartache that was on the earth that made me appreciate what I was seeing in the future. I saw mothers who were frantically looking for their children and for their babies who were suddenly missing. They were looking to see if they were lost or if they had been kidnapped. I had a sense that the children and babies were being transported with me along with many others who were leaving the earth.

Many people had adult loved ones who were missing. They were leaving the earth and traveling beyond the atmosphere. As

David E. Siriano

I was looking ahead to what was happening in front of me I still had the sense that behind me disaster was striking the world as people were absent everywhere. People who would normally be at work, didn't show up. Leaders of many countries and those in governmental positions were all of a sudden missing. Fear, turmoil and confusion gripped everyone's lives all around the world. Automobiles, planes, trucks and buses were destroyed. Accidents happened on the job as everyone's lives were being upset by the fear and disasters. People on earth were disturbed and they were weeping as they ran from home to home, searching for loved ones and friends. I knew all these things in an instant.

With the hopelessness that was happening behind me, I was still looking ahead as my body was definitely being changed. I knew it. It felt light and filled with a weightless pleasure. I went through a spiritual change that no one could understand unless they went through the same process that I was going through. I was no longer encumbered with earthly worries and fears. All of my misgivings were gone. My mind and heart were full of hope and now open to all kinds of spiritual understanding. The only way that I could describe it was that it felt as if my mind that was once filled with cobwebs was now swept and clean of all its impurities. I felt renewed in my spirit.

I remembered a scripture I heard as a child in Sunday school that my teacher said that the Apostle Paul wrote about the future resurrection for all who were believers in Christ. Paul said, *"The body is sown in corruption, it is raised in incorruption. It is sown in dishonor, it is raised in glory. It is sown in weakness, it is raised in power. It is sown a natural body, it is raised a spiritual body."* I felt that I was now living in that kind of victory. I was so relieved and comforted as I passed beyond time and beyond the pull of gravity.

Still, questions filled my mind. I was so inquisitive. Where was I? Was I going to heaven? What would I see? Was I in a sane

15

state of mind? It wasn't long after those questions blurred my thinking that I then saw another brilliant light that was far more unimaginable than I had ever known before. It was a light that was different and far brighter than the sun that had shone on the earth. It was brighter than any light that I had seen so far on this spiritual journey that I was on. I wasn't blinded by it and it didn't hurt my eyes but it penetrated my mind and soul and what I think was this spiritual body that I now had. The light that I saw made everything appear clear and white as far as the eye could see. I felt such release, such peace and pureness of thought as I just knew that I was in the holy presence of God. I wasn't scared but I was filled with a holy awe and presence.

My past life on earth mattered little at this point. I would never have wanted to go back anyway. I saw my brothers and sisters who were here. I also saw friends that had preceded me to heaven. I saw my grandparents and also my mother and father that had raised me to serve the Lord. I then saw my wife and family and I was relieved and overjoyed. Now I knew that they were fine. A great thrill and happiness filled my being. After a brief time of recognition of each other, I quickly passed them by as I was in what appeared to be a tremendous large room. It probably wasn't a room but it was like a presence or beautiful atmosphere that encased me and enhanced me with love, mercy, grace, forgiveness, brightness and glory. I felt a heavenly closeness to God that I never felt before. I was in heaven!

PRESENCE OF GOD

I saw this bright shining light and I knew that I was seeing God as He appeared right in front of me. It was indescribable. He couldn't be ignored or evaded. No one could hide from Him. It was God! I felt like melting in this close encounter with Him. I was respectful and humbled before Him as I sensed the inside of me being torn apart and every thought that I ever had on earth was being exposed. The others that I had just seen, had they been here with me as well? Were they feeling the same things that I was feeling?

Before the answer came to my mind, all of a sudden I was on my knees in front of a great throne in heaven as none of my sins that I vaguely remembered seem to grip me. They were gone as a strange but powerful holiness and righteousness burned inside me. I felt purged by a holy fire and cleansed within. The force of God's forgiveness came to me as the promise in His word says, *"As far as the east is from the west, So far has He removed our transgressions from us. As a father pities his children, so the LORD PITIES THOSE WHO FEAR HIM. For He knows our frame; He remembers that we are dust."* I was dwelling in a state of forgiveness.

Then I knew that I was not alone. All of the others that I sensed moments ago were there as well. I could tell by how they were enthralled by God's presence that they too knew that their sins were forgiven. I had been translated with them and all of us had a deep understanding that we were cleansed from our evil past as we stood in front of the throne of the Heavenly Father. Everything where we were was a brilliant white that reflected the holiness of the state of the spirit we were in.

The likeness of Christ was at God's right hand as Christ was in view on His left side as I looked at the throne. I knew that it was Jesus because I heard many times in my lifetime that it was Jesus who sat at *"the right hand of God."* I now experienced what it was like to behold Him! I sensed what the disciples must have felt when they saw Christ after His resurrection! What a glorious and astounding sense of the presence of God! We were in heaven forever!

My thoughts went back to all of the preaching I heard about the book of Revelation. I recalled many of the things it said as they all now raced through my mind. While still on the earth I remembered that there would be a blessing from God to those who read and heard the teachings of the book of Revelation. That was exciting as those words were still impacting my life. I remember reading that it said *"Blessed* is *he that reads, and they that hear the words of this prophecy, and keep those things which are written therein: for the time* is *at hand."*

When I thought about it on earth I knew that surely God was going to remember me and bless me for my efforts even though I really couldn't explain or understand all of it. That promised blessing from God not only influenced me on earth but it was now embracing me in heaven. I needed to become aware of all of this and all of my surroundings with my spiritual eyes.

The book of Revelation made it clear that the Apostle John wrote about the future events that were recorded in it. I remember that he was on an island and had plenty of time for God to reveal Himself as he faithfully wrote down everything that he saw. In his message to the seven churches, he was greatly moved in the Spirit with tremendous and numerous visions that he received from God.

He spoke about the seven-fold manifestation of the Holy Spirit that was in front of the throne of God. I do remember hearing that the seven-fold Spirit was the Spirit of the Lord, wisdom, understanding, counsel, might, knowledge, and the fear of the Lord. What a blessing it was to understand this ministry that had been sent by Jesus Christ to the people of God on earth.

John also saw Jesus Christ and wrote that His presence was known throughout all of the Christian world at that time. I now was able to see what he had written about. What he wrote was glorious and beyond my earthly comprehension! I do remember that He said that indeed the Spirit of Jesus Christ was present in every church that held to and preached the name of Jesus Christ.

He described the church on earth as the ones who were washed from their sins in His blood and would one day be around the throne in heaven to be with the Lord eternally. John viewed the people of the church on earth as being the ones that in the future would reign with Jesus Christ on earth as *"kings and priests."* Thank God I was now in Heaven with the church just as John had predicted.

I realized more than ever now that I was in heaven, that the Lord was the one who was going to return to earth to reveal Himself as God. As it says, *"Behold, He is coming with clouds, and every eye will see Him, even they who pierced Him. And all the tribes of the earth will mourn because of Him. Even so, Amen. I am the Alpha and the Omega, the Beginning and the End," says the Lord, "who is and who was and who is to come, the Almighty."*

I now saw things that were revealed to me like never before. What I didn't understand on earth when I read the book of Revelation, I was now comprehending in heaven. What John had detailed on earth I was now seeing in heaven. I knew in an instant that the Priestly work in the Bible was truly a shadow of heavenly things. I caught a glimpse of Christ in heaven in all of the glory that God the Father gave to Him.

Jesus was described by John as having Priestly robes. I saw the beauty of His ministry that was given to Him. I remember while reading the Old Testament that it was the role of the Priest to bring the people to God in prayer and that's what Jesus was doing even as I saw Him with my eternal eyes. It was true, Jesus was interceding for the world. I remembered even greater now what the Bible said that He lives in heaven to make *"intercession for us"*.

MY EYES SAW JESUS

I saw Jesus and He was real to me like never before and ever so close to me in the Spirit realm. I loved His presence and basked in it as pictures of His entire ministry were revealed to me and also to all who were in heaven with me. Everything about Him spoke volumes to me of His life and ministry when He was on earth but especially now that I was in heaven with Him. When I saw Him I felt like the two who met Jesus after His resurrection when He spoke the scriptures to them. The two of them said, *"Did not our heart burn within us while He talked with us on the road, and while He opened the Scriptures to us?"*

As I looked at those Priestly robes again that John described, I saw them as if they came all the way down to His feet. To me they were symbolic of His ministry. They glistened with a beauty that pierced my heart and soul. I sensed a belt around His body that spoke to me of the strength of His service and work for all of humanity in the world. I saw the purity, fatherhood and eternity of His divine life in the whiteness of His hair that was radiant with Divine glory. He had eyes of fire that penetrated my very being. His feet appeared to be like brass in color and seemed to be treading heavily in a manner that would annihilate evil. All of His clothing that I saw were symbols of His Divine Ministry.

I heard His voice and it flowed out of Him like waters of grace, beauty, and salvation. It spoke volumes to all of the listeners in heaven. With His voice came what appeared to be a powerful sword from His mouth to cut through any mistrust and misgivings I may have had. The words that He spoke penetrated my body, soul, and spirit. The glow around His being was bright with glory as every one of His marvelous attributes and characteristics seemed to cover me as a waterfall. His brightness was brilliant. I was in awe of His presence and might. I couldn't move as I was struck with motionless silence and respect. We were in the presence of the Almighty God and His Son Jesus Christ who gave His life for all of our sins!

Christ was standing among the churches yet seemed to be holding the churches and the people of the churches in the palms of His hands. I don't know how that was possible but that was the reality that I sensed. Hell and death were banished from His sight as I heard the proclamation from His own lips that He was *"the first and the last"* and that He held the *"keys of hell and of death"*. He had power over hell and death so that He would be able to deliver anyone He chose to deliver. He could keep people out of hell or lock people in hell. It would depend on whether or not they had believed in Him and whether or not they had trusted and lived for God in their lifetime on earth.

Not only were the churches and the people of the churches in His hand, He also had the leaders of the churches in His hand as well. They were all now in heaven and were the ones who would receive rewards for all of their Godly work. I was stunned with amazement as my initial response was to want to hide from Him who sat on the throne and the Christ who was at His right hand, but His grace released me to absorb His presence. I felt at ease and was reassured of His kindness and mercy.

Chapter Two: Ephesus, Smyrna, Pergamos, Thyatira

T he churches that Christ had power and sway with were not buildings or temples, they were people that were immersed in His love and sense of forgiveness. They had trusted in the message of the Cross of Christ and the power of His resurrection that would bring them resurrection as well. The saved people of those churches were now in heaven. They all had eternal life that they anticipated so much. I saw them and I was with them enjoying all of the benefits of heaven.

It was revealed to me that the seven churches that were mentioned in the book of Revelation were example of the massive amount of believers that had encountered the living God throughout all of the world and in all periods of time. On earth they were the churches that were filled with real worshippers at the time that the book of Revelation was written, but they also represented the next two thousand years of worshippers as well. There had been an emphasis of different biblical theology throughout the centuries but they were people from all walks of life and from every culture and from many different doctrinal understandings.

These were the churches and the people that made an impact throughout the world. They spanned all of history since the time of Christ. All of their differences of race, culture and doctrine didn't seem to matter in heaven. They were God's people and He was their God and they were now before Him and His throne.

I was able to look back in time over the past two thousand years and saw that they overcame periods of struggle that I could not even fathom or understand. It seemed like Christ knew and understood them all and had compassion on them. He was merciful and gracious to them all. I saw myriads of people that were now in heaven who were victorious despite the struggles, persecution, and martyrdom by many in their time of existence on earth. They had faithfully served God and were now enjoying His presence.

While on earth the Lord had something good or bad to say about each of the churches. He gave them counsel and He challenged them. Now that they were in heaven they were the overcomers that He mentioned they could be if they were faithful to Him. They are now a church in heaven without spot or wrinkle as the Bible said. I knew that they were free of any moral blemish. I was mesmerized by the closeness that Christ had with what would be His Bride, the church.

Missionaries that I knew that had travelled from church to church during my lifetime as well as Pastors and leaders of past history that were now in heaven helped me to understand what those churches were like. I also met the Pastors that were ministering during the time of the book of Revelation and they were now in heaven. For some reason I was able to see what the churches were like through their eyes as well. I knew that everyone could live any or all of the life changing principles that God had revealed to these seven churches throughout history and be blessed of God. This was a time of great rejoicing for the church of Jesus Christ in heaven. What a wonderful time it was to hear them all share their testimonies with each other.

A Look Beyond

EPHESUS

The people of the church of **Ephesus** in history were now in heaven enjoying the love of God. Christ encouraged them by telling them that He was the one who held the leaders of all the churches in His hand and He walked among all of the seven churches.

I met Polycrates who was a Christian Pastor in Ephesus at that time and was a leader in the church there. He spoke to me of the teachings and traditions of the Apostle John that were still fresh in everyone's mind at the time of his birth. He introduced me to many of the saints of God from that church who rose from the dead and were now in heaven. They had been anxiously waiting for Christ when He was to come for all of the saints. He was a man who was deeply in love with the Lord. He said to me, "I lived for the Lord for over sixty-five years and I exchanged testimony with brethren from all over the world." His expression was one of excitement and love for all of them. He further said about persecution, "We read and taught the scriptures with each other and knew that we had to obey God rather than man."

Ephesus was a church that knew how to detect false prophets. The Lord knew about their strong work ethic and their patience, but it was their gift of discerning of spirits that really benefited the church as they separated themselves from evil. At that time there were some who claimed to be Apostles of the Lord but the church had discerned that they were liars. They showed their perseverance, they endured hardships and did not grow weary. They worked hard at preaching in the name of Jesus Christ and had much fruit for their labor.

There was one thing however that the Lord was upset with them about. They were not in a close relationship with the Lord as they once were. It was the fact that many of them had lost their love that they first had with Him and did not repent and were now lost. They would be separated from God for eternity. God even threatened to remove their candlestick which was a representation of their church. He said that they would be remembered no more and that they would not have the opportunity of being in heaven. God told them to go back and do the first things that brought them to the Lord such as their personal honor and behavior, and discovering the influence that they originally had in their community.

The Lord was happy that they had nothing to do with a certain group of teachers of their time which were a counterfeit leadership group. They were really out to destroy the relationship that the people had with Christ. These false leaders would encourage people to live a life that was full of worshipping the things of the world and not worshipping Christ.

Those who did repent were the remnant of that type of church and were free and deeply in love with Christ. They were now overcomers that were in heaven to enjoy the tree of life that is in God's paradise. This tree of life is what will be revealed in the New Heaven and New Earth once time on earth is no more. Eating of the tree of life is what gives eternity to them. It grew near the water of life that came from the throne of God and from the Lamb. They were now in the throne room of God enjoying His peace and refreshment.

SMYRNA

The people of the church of **Smyrna** were also enjoying the benefits of being in the throne room of God. The Lord had told them that He was the First and the Last. In other words He was to them both the beginning of everything that was in the past and He was also the ending of everything that was going to be in the future. He reminded them that at one time He had died for their sins on Calvary but that He was also the one who was resurrected after being three days and three nights in the tomb.

A Look Beyond

They were rich in spirit and had much to be thankful for as they were delivered from the many hardships of presenting the Gospel during the existence of their church. They were aware of the counterfeit Jews who attempted to worship with them but who were really working as the devises of the Devil. Christ knew about the evil works of these imposters.

This church had lived through many trials and persecutions in various parts of the world and in many times in history, particularly in the first couple of hundred years of the life of the church on earth. He said that they were going to suffer many things and even go to prison during years of tribulation throughout those early centuries. These persecutions and times of tribulation took place during the first 300 years of the church and involved 10 different Roman Emperors who killed many of them. It was awful as there were many Antichrists who harassed the church.

In heaven, I met Polycarp from that church. He had been a disciple of John and was ordained by him as a Pastor of the church at Smyrna. He spoke numerous times with John and many others who had seen Jesus Christ and heard the words He spoke to them. He then related to me the terrible experience that was his martyrdom. "They took me from my home and tied me with ropes to burn me at a large stake. All because I believed in Jesus Christ and His resurrection power. I could not escape."

"There was no one to help you," I asked? "No one" he said. He went on to say, "The flames were as hot as the fires of hell itself. I could not breathe. Miraculously the fire did not burn me as it eventually died out. They roughly pulled me from the stake and stabbed me repeatedly until my spirit left my body. They were unmerciful as the knives were thrust into my chest and eventually reached my heart. The pain was immense but I was released from my body to be in the presence of the Lord." He told me that the pain was excruciating, but I saw him and was now talking to him as he was joyfully sharing in the glories of heaven.

Many others from that church who kept their walk with Christ perfect were now enjoying the crown of life and would not be touched by the second death which is an eternity separated from God. God has blessed them with eternal life. Christ found no fault with this church because they grew in God's Word during extreme times of persecution and martyrdom and were extremely faithful to the cause of Christ.

PERGAMOS

Many who belonged to the church of **Pergamos** remained faithful and true to the Lord's name. The Lord that had the two-edged sword who would annihilate their enemies, was the one who was speaking to them. Many of the people of this church did not deny their faith even though a prominent disciple of the Lord was martyred in this satanic prevalent city at a place called 'Satan's Seat'.

Now that I was in heaven I met that martyr. His name is Antipas. While we were standing near the throne he revealed to me what happened to him. I asked, "How were you martyred?" He said, "I was slowly roasted alive in a bronze kettle with a bonfire underneath." I told him that I couldn't imagine going through that kind of torture. "Why did it happen," I asked? He said "I would not compromise what I believed in and that is what cost me my life. They tried to get me to recant my beliefs but I remained a faithful witness for Jesus and stayed true to my testimony." It was beautiful as he said that he would not give in to his tormentors even unto the point of death. What an amazing story of faithfulness to the Lord.

However, there were some of this church who were caught up in the worship of idols and are now lost forever like in the Old

Testament time of Balaam who taught idolatry. Some in this church did not follow the truth of who Christ is. The Lord did not like the fact that they allowed a certain group of teachers in the church who were a counterfeit leadership group that were out to destroy the people's relationship with Christ. They were told to repent or the Lord would come and fight against them with the sword that would come out of His mouth.

Many people were victorious over the ravages of the Devil. All of the overcomers in this era of the church were now in heaven and enjoying the fellowship of being with Christ and eating of the heavenly bread that only He can give. These faithful Christians were given a personal white stone of acceptance. A name known only to them was written on it to show the strong bond they have in their new position in the heavenly Kingdom. They are forever alive in the presence of God at His throne.

THYATIRA

The people of the church of **Thyatira** all were people who performed works of love, service, faith, and patience. The Lord who was speaking to them had penetrating eyes like fire that could see into and through anything, and who also had feet like brass of judgment. Christ commended them for all that they did.

However, He also chided them for allowing those who were examples of fornication and idolatry to teach and remain in their midst. They were false prophets that led the people to stray away from the true teaching of the Lord. One of them was a wicked woman symbolically referred to as Jezebel who is now suffering in the fires of hell for her deceitfulness. She, like the wicked Jezebel of the Old Testament promoted the idolatrous and immoral worship of Baal. This Jezebel of Thyatira in the New Testament, regarded herself as a Christian prophetess. She was a shameful example of how an imposter could lead other people away from the true teachings of the Lord.

The Lord gave them time to repent but they did not. Those who continued to live in this evil behavior and those who followed them would be going through the Great Tribulation. Because of their satanic connection they would miss heaven. Those who repented would be able to miss the horrible time on earth that was surely going to come. The Lord who knew their works is the one who searched and knew their hearts. He told them to hold on to their faith.

Many people of this time overcame idols and martyrdom and the ravages of seducing spirits. Men of God such as Pastor SS Carpus and his Deacon Papylus suffered horribly during this time. They would not celebrate the pagan festivals that were held there each year in Thyatira. They were threatened to either become involved with their rituals or be killed. Pastor Carpus told those who represented the Emperor Decius, "It would be improper for us to worship false gods." Both he and his Deacon were tied to horses and dragged to the city of Sardis. They beheaded them both there.

These were among those who overcame much of the evil of their generation and were given the promise that they would rule the nations, breaking them in pieces. They are with me now rejoicing in heaven and clinging to the promise of knowing that they will rule with Christ with a rod of iron during a beautiful future Millennium of 1,000 years on earth. They are basking with the 'morning star' which is the light of Christ and the Gospel message.

Chapter Three: Sardis, Philadelphia, Laodicea

SARDIS

There were some people who lived in the era of the church in **Sardis** that were numb and dead to the things of God, but the church had a reputation that they were living a great life serving God. The Lord who possessed the seven-fold manifestation of the Spirit of God and who held the seven leaders of the churches in His hand is the one who was speaking to them. They were a spiritually lifeless church that tolerated sin. They did nothing about the sin that was so prevalent among them. They did not know how mistaken they were and their works showed that they were not perfect. Christ told them to repent. Many missed the translation to heaven and had to wait until the end of the tribulation when Christ would come to the world as a thief.

However, there were some in this church age who truly lived a pure life and they were given the promise of wearing white clothing which showed their righteousness. One such man was Clement, Pastor of the church of Sardis. He was a disciple of the Apostle Paul and was faithful to the work of God.

The overcomers in this church would have their names kept in the book of life. Christ would confess them before the Father who sat on the throne and before the angels of God in heaven. Those promises were fulfilled as many who were ready to meet the Lord were translated, and are now with Christ and the Heavenly Father in heaven. They are enjoying an eternity filled with these promises and other promises as well.

PHILADELPHIA

Those who belonged to the church of **Philadelphia** walked through an open door in strength because they kept God's word and did not deny the name of Christ. The one who spoke to the people of this church was the one who was holy and true. It was Christ and He had the key of David. That meant that He had the power and the authority that could open and shut the door that would lead to all of the covenant blessings of the Kingdom of God. This door was right in front of them and they could walk right through it if they wanted to with the strength they had.

Some of them of this era still lied and said they were Jews who were believers but God knew that they were not. They left the safety of the worship of God to follow the wiles of the Devil. These evil ones would come and fall at the feet of the true believers and worship God in order to prove that God loved the people of this church that were true and faithful to the Lord.

Despite all of that, this was a church that Christ found no fault with because of their great love. Because they obeyed the word of God, they were kept from going through the time of the Great Tribulation that Christ said would come upon the whole world. This tribulation was a time of severe temptation for all of those who missed the translation of the church to heaven.

I met many of them from that church and they were now in heaven as the pillars of strength in the Temple of God which is His holy presence. They would never have to leave the place of sanctuary around God's throne. The Lord has written on them a new name which is the name of God and the name of the city of God on their life and personalities. They are never to be removed and are now enjoying the blessings of God.

LAODICEA

The church of the time of **Laodicea** was a church that was spoken to by Jesus Christ who was the Amen, the faithful and true witness of God. He was there in the beginning of all creation with the Father. He knew their works and they were not in the place that they should have been in their relationship with the Lord.

This church was filled with much compromise because they lived a life of pretense. They were a fake. They were neither hot for God nor cold for God. They were lukewarm and therefore complacent in their walk with Him.

This was a church filled with disaster. They made no sacrifices for the Kingdom of God. They thought that they were rich and needed nothing, but deep down they were pitiful, miserable, poor, blind, and naked. Christ told them that they had to walk through the fires of persecution so that they could be rich in the Lord. He also told them that they needed to clothe themselves with the pure white garments so that they would not be spiritually naked. He said that they needed to anoint their eyes that they could see the error of their ways. They were told to repent. Christ loved them and told them that He wanted to rebuke and chastise them.

He was knocking at the door of their hearts but they would not open up to Him and let Him in. Christ wanted to come into their lives to live and fellowship with them. There were some who were overcomers and they were now in heaven with Christ. They were obedient and followed the ways of the Lord. They were now with the Heavenly Father in His throne room enjoying the blessings of God.

The one wonderful thing about the church is that there was a man by the name of Nymphas who permitted the early church to meet in his house in Laodicea. I met him here in heaven and he was now rejoicing in the Lord. I was curious about this church and I asked him about its horrible condition and how it ended up the way that it did. His response was "I am so sorrowful that the church that I knew started off so spiritual, had strayed far away from God because it compromised with the world." He was heartsick.

Another man I met here in heaven who was deeply troubled about the church was a man by the name of Archippus who had a great ministry in the church of Colossae and was a friend of those at Laodicea. He was living in joy but he too felt very grieved. He said, "I watched the church over the years and couldn't understand their complacency that led the church to such a lukewarm condition." He knew of the godly sorrow that brings repentance, but in this case he felt the sorrow that worked death in the lives of those at Laodicea.

THE CHURCH AROUND THE THRONE

I was in the throne room of God with the millions upon millions of people of the church who were now blessed of God and around His Throne. God gave me a bird's eye view of the entire area of heaven and I saw the people of all of those churches in every quarter praising God and worshipping His holy Name. Their praise was ecstatic as it reverberated throughout the entire heavens. It was a sight to behold!

No matter where we were in heaven all of us felt that we were close to the Throne of God. You could be what seemed to be miles away from the throne yet could still feel the presence of God everywhere. Even though it seemed we were far from the throne it was as if we were standing right next to it. I can't explain it any other way. It was amazing! Everyone felt close to

A Look Beyond

the Throne of God the Father. There was a fellowship with Him that sat on the throne that was indescribable. What a thrill to see all of those gathered together to be free from the things that had encumbered them in their existence on earth.

All of the people of the entire church throughout history who were overcomers in all things in their walk with Christ were the ones that I now viewed in heaven. Because they were the ones who were overcomers, they were the ones now enjoying the benefits of the tree of life in which they will live forever. They felt the assurance that they will never die again! They were eating of the manna of God which was their eternal life. They were free from any accusation of sin with a new name given to them by God. They had the promise of God that they were to rule over the nations in the new Kingdom of God.

They were now clothed in white to show their marriage to Christ for eternity and had their names written in the book of life. They were the foundation and strength of the Temple of God in eternity. They were now part of the Throne of God in His rule and authority. They were at peace, and praise God I was now a part of that group! Those promises were mine to fathom and enjoy as well! To God be Praise!

Chapter Four: Around the Throne

T he Throne of God! What amazement! What a spectacular sense of spiritual enlightenment and vision that I never knew existed! There was the Heavenly Father on the throne of the universe and all of eternity, and I was standing in front of that glorious and marvelous throne! I was struck with awe!

When I looked at the Father his appearance of brilliance, graciousness and beauty took on every color of the rainbow. The glory of God reflected off of a transparent sea of glass in front of the throne representing His purity and holiness that moved unlimited throughout the heavens. Everyone was impacted by the preeminence and brightness of the Creator of the universe. I talked to Moses who was standing next to me and he spoke to me about it as he had written in the Old Testament when he *"... saw the God of Israel. And there was under His feet as it were a paved work of sapphire stone, and it was like the very heavens in its clarity."*

What a difference between now and the time of Moses on the earth. Moses had asked to see the glory of God while he was leading the children of Israel through the wilderness. God said yes, but he was only allowed to see the back side of God because God's glory was too bright and would have killed him. Now

A Look Beyond

Moses and all of us were in the presence of God and we sensed His life and glory. Any veil of darkness and misunderstanding had now disappeared for all of us who were there. I saw Moses approach the throne and I knew that he was looking at all of the glory of God. What a thrill it was to know that Moses' request to see the glory of God had been fulfilled ever since he had arrived in heaven. He had been here a lot longer than I was, but for me to see the satisfaction on his face was priceless!

The personality of the Father who sat on the throne appeared as gorgeous rays of light revealed to me as two of the most precious gemstone colors that I could ever imagine. They were most beautiful in their appearance as a mix of red, yellow, blue, green, and purple haze with a flesh tint. I knew that God is not made of flesh but these colors radiated a stunning array of brightness that far surpassed what I had seen on earth. Their appearances were separate yet beautifully blended. This was the glory of God in the highest of splendor and magnificence.

I was stunned as the revelation came to me that those very colors were connected to the nation of Israel through the Old Testament Priest. They were the same as the first and last stones in the breastplate that the High Priest wore. They represented Judah's firstborn 'Reuben' and his lastborn 'Benjamin'. Their names meant "Behold a Son" and "Son of my right hand". I got the sense that just like Jesus explained to Philip that if you've seen Jesus you would have seen the Heavenly Father, so I also knew that now that I've seen the Heavenly Father I have seen Jesus.

As I saw them both it was as if they were of one desire and purpose so that no one who sincerely came to God would be lost but that all would come to know who they were. That was the purpose of Christ's ministry on the earth. Their desire and will for the world to know who God the Father was, and who the Son of God was, were of identical purpose. It was as Jesus said, "*I seek not mine own will, but the will of the Father which hath sent me,"* and also, **"***...no one knows the Son except the Father. Nor does anyone know the Father except the Son...***"** It was just like I was taught in my Sunday school classes.

There was a rainbow around the throne of the Heavenly Father that was green in color. That was the color of the tribe of Judah in Israel through which Jesus the Messiah came. It was as if God had this whole throne room scene planned in unity with His Son for all of eternity. Was there some special meaning to all of the colors surrounding the Heavenly Father and identifying Him with the nation of Israel? Did Israel have some special part in all of the events that were coming in the book of Revelation? I was hoping that God would help me to understand all of my questions.

TWENTY-FOUR ELDERS AND FOUR CREATURES

In and around the throne were twenty-four Elders that were sitting on twenty-four thrones as the representatives of the people of God that were translated to heaven. All of them were wearing white garments and had crowns of gold on their heads. Lightning, thundering and voices came from the throne, as I saw there seven lights of fire that represented the seven Spirits of God. I once again knew in an instant that they were the seven manifestations of the one Holy Spirit that was with God and in His throne that John had written about.

As I took in the peripheral landscape of the Throne of God I then realized even stronger than before that I was not alone. Around me were the millions of individuals as represented by the twenty-four Elders that were just as enthralled with God as I was. They were full of joy and relief with what I can only describe as smiles not on their faces, but smiles in their souls. That's the only way that I could describe the depth of the happiness that I felt emanating from deep within all of us.

A Look Beyond

The most complex and inexplicable thing that I saw in and around the throne were four Living Creatures. They were simply amazing to me. They had the appearance of a lion, calf, man, and an eagle. They had six wings. With two wings they covered their feet to acknowledge their respect for the holy area around the throne, with two they covered their eyes to acknowledge the excellence of His glory, and with two they flew around the throne to declare His honor. They were full of eyes that were able to observe everything in heaven. What were they and what did they stand for? Why were they there?

It seemed to me that they had the dual role of spiritual beings such as angels protecting the throne, but possessed a beautiful excellence and wonderful characteristics of earthly beings. They possessed earthly reminders of the strength of a lion, the service of a calf, the wisdom and knowledge of a man, and the swiftness of an eagle, all in obedience to the commands of God. They were heavenly representatives associated with the redemption of man on earth that I took to represent the Cherubim and Seraphim angels of God seen in the Bible.

I heard them as they continued to say over and over again, *"Holy, holy, holy, Lord God Almighty, which was, and is, and is to come."* It was an echoing and piercing pronouncement that no one grew tired of hearing. They continued saying it over and over again and we felt that we could listen to it for eternity. We were in heaven because the holiness and righteousness of God that inspired love and forgiveness for His creation brought us to the throne!

Their characteristics also seemed to reflect the ministry and power of Christ in the New Testament. A sweeping assurance came over me that these four living creatures were angels of God that were there to carry on the ministry of God before the throne just like Christ did while He was on earth. I got the impression that they not only executed the will of Him who sat on the throne, but that they would be fulfilling the future affairs of the Kingdom of God on earth during the Millennium. That's why they looked like the earthly creatures that they personified.

Now was the time for rewards and judgment for our works as we stood in front of Christ. I remembered what the scripture had said that *"we shall all stand before the judgment seat of Christ."* Line after line of individuals came before the throne as all of us were honest in the assessment of our own lives, as the spotlight of God shined upon all who stood before the all-seeing eyes of God. God didn't have to say anything to us and we didn't have to say anything to God. God was living so powerfully in us that each of us felt the burning sensation that everything was open and raw within us. God knew everything! There wasn't a thing that could be hid from Him. I was relieved of all my wrongdoing of the past as a pureness in my spirit enveloped me.

Our heart, conscience and thoughts were open books. Our words and secrets could not be contained. I felt that some things inside me had been good and some things seemed not so good. It didn't matter because all of the seemingly not so good things were all gone from within me. Everything was out in the open. Rewards were meted out for our works as crowns were given to all who served God in their individual capacity. I had remembered the powerful words of the Apostle Paul who wrote that *"Every man's work shall be made manifest: for the day shall declare it, because it shall be revealed by fire; and the fire shall try every man's work of what sort it is."*

These were the ones who were saved but everyone had to give an account of the worthiness of their works. They had to tell of their faithfulness to God's Word, their Christ-like attitude, their soul-winning, how they overcame temptation, and even the use of their time and money. They came to the throne with the souls they won to Christ. A great rejoicing echoed through heaven every time a soul was accounted for. All Christians were judged on a number of things they did while they were Christians on earth.

THE CROWNS

Then I saw the crowns! They were indescribably awesome as I looked at them up close even though at first I was far from them. They were beautiful and striking in their appearance. It did not appear that they were made with any kind of earthly substance. It seemed that they were sculpted with the brightness of earthly stones, yet were not made of earthly stones. They were brilliant in color as they were placed on our heads by angels. They seemed to become eternally meshed with our spiritual bodies. I really couldn't explain it but it seemed that they couldn't be separated from us. They were ours eternally. It was like they were permanently attached and couldn't be removed. The only time they were removed was when we cast them at the foot of the Throne of God in reverence and thankfulness, and we did that often.

Everyone received the crown of life which meant that we would live forever in God's eternal heavenly kingdom. Some received the crown that was incorruptible because they were exceptional overcomers of their old nature of sin and now their corrupt ways were gone. Their lives were not in a corruptible state anymore. Some received the crown of rejoicing because they caused others to become believers in Christ. They were rejoicing and were wise because of their soul winning.

I was reminded of the Old Testament Proverb that said, "*He that winneth souls is wise.*" They reflected the heavenly attitude of being skillful and prudent by ministering the will of the Heavenly Father that as many as possible could come to heaven and be saved from the treachery of hell. I felt more than ever before that the Lord is "*not willing that any should perish, but that all should come to repentance.*"

David E. Siriano

Many were given the crown of righteousness because they had looked and waited patiently for the coming of Christ and now were righteous like Him. Finally, Pastor after Pastor, and Godly teachers, all stood in front of the throne to receive the crown of glory because they remained faithful to their God-called ministry and were now basking in God's glory.

Each of the twenty-four Elders then took the crowns from off their heads and threw them down before the Heavenly Father on the throne. It was as if they were feeling what I was feeling that none of us were worthy of any reward that God would give us. We were only there because of the love and grace of God that permeated our very being. The unworthiness of Gods mercy in all of our lives seemed to envelope us with waves of thankfulness and gratitude.

All of the heavenly creatures had joined the twenty four elders in honoring God for His glory and power. Then, all of us joined the twenty-four Elders in casting our crowns at the feet of our eternal Heavenly Father and worshiped Him. We were all rejoicing because of the special relationship we now had with Him as the creator of all things. It was because of Him and for Him and His pleasure that all things were created. What a time of blessing it was for all of us as we knelt before Him who sat on the throne and who lives forever and ever.

Chapter Five: The Lion and the Lamb

Then something unfolded before me for which I had no answer. The Heavenly Father on the throne was holding a book in His right hand in appearance as a scroll that was sealed shut with seven seals. It was similar to a governmental sealed book that could only be opened by the proper authorities. I was told by an angel that God had the rights to the possession of the book and that no one had the power or the life of Divine holiness to take it from His hand and reveal its contents. He had control over the book and what was written in it. I was told it represented His authority over the earth. That didn't surprise me at all because I remembered a Psalm that said, "*The earth is the LORD's, AND ALL ITS FULLNESS, THE WORLD AND THOSE WHO DWELL THEREIN.*"

I was in a state of wonder because no one could open it. I was appalled. There was much weeping in heaven because everyone wanted to know what was in the book. Everyone was crying from one side of heaven to the other. They wanted to see its contents brought forth but it was announced that no one was allowed to view what was in it. Everyone was flabbergasted, including myself. What was in the book? What was God holding back from us? Were there blessings in it or would the anger of

God be kindled through it in curses and wrath? Would He rescue the world or was He going to let it go through grave punishment? I wasn't sure even though I had read about the wrath of God in the book of Revelation.

I thought, why couldn't the one who sat on the throne open it? Why couldn't the Father of the entire universe open the book? Apparently, someone other than Him had to open it because He had to remain on the throne. An inquiry went out through the heavens to open it but no one was found. No one in heaven or no one on earth or no one who had been on earth could open it. A representative of the Father had to open it. Someone who had His Divine nature and His best interests at heart had to open it. Someone He could trust and who could help Him redeem the earth had to open it.

Then one of the Elders said that the *"The Lion of the tribe of Judah"* had the authority to open the book and reveal its contents. I felt relief and comfort because I knew that the Lion of the Tribe of Judah was none other than the Son of the one who sat on the throne, Jesus Christ! He was born as part of the tribe of Judah and was the only one who was righteous enough to follow the commands of the Heavenly Father.

When we turned to look at Him it seemed as if a marvelous transformation took place because we didn't see a Lion at all. All of us saw a Lamb, and He was right in the middle of the Throne of God. He was part of the Godhead. It looked as if the Lamb had been killed but yet it was still alive. I then immediately sensed that it too represented Christ, but in the form of the crucified and slain Son of God. It was at this moment that the Holy Spirit spoke to me of the powerful scripture that said *"the blood of Jesus Christ his Son cleanseth us from all sin."*

He was being revealed to us as being slain yet alive, who had died for the sins of the world, and yet would redeem the world in this moment of wrath. He had seven horns and seven eyes which also represented the seven manifestations of the Spirit of God that I knew was right there with us. Whatever was about to happen would come from the very heart and center of God Himself.

IT IS JESUS

Everyone started rejoicing in Heaven. They were proclaiming, "It's Jesus, it is Jesus"! Everyone started shouting and singing praises because of the victorious life, death and resurrection of Christ that brought so many people into the very presence of God. I remembered the words of Jesus that He spoke when He was on earth, *"I am the resurrection and the life. He who believes in me, though he may die, he shall live."* I was thrilled with this memory that gave strength to my eternity. I was in heaven forever.

Then I saw Jesus the Lamb approach the throne of the Father and take the book from His hand. I found out that the book that the Lamb took were the judgments that were to begin the Great Tribulation. These were a complete series of seven judgments that the earth was about to endure. These judgments were sealed shut and only Christ could open them. I thought to myself that I was glad that I was in heaven and not on the earth. I stood there in amazement as I wondered how these judgments would unfold when He opened the book.

I realized that the judgments did not come from Christ's work as a Lion, but from His work as a Lamb. The wrath from the throne of God will not come from the viciousness of a Lion that could tear the world apart, but from the mercy of the Lamb that could bring judgment with compassion. It would be from His mercy and grace that He would allow wrath to come upon the earth in order for restoration to take place. Only the Father and Jesus had the right to exercise these judgments upon the earth. After all, they are the ones who have the ownership of the world and of the universe.

It was God the Father and Jesus the Son that created the worlds as the scripture says, *"God, who at various times and in various ways spoke in time past to the fathers by the prophets, has in these last days spoken to us by His Son, whom He has appointed heir of all things, through whom also He made the worlds."* They were the ones who had the right to bring judgment upon it. The sealed book was about to be opened.

I saw the twenty-four Elders and the four Living Creatures bow down before the Lamb. The twenty-four Elders represented the redeemed people who were now in heaven. They were our representatives before the throne. Even the four Living Creatures who were angels of God also joined in with the redemptive chorus because they possessed the earthly expressions of the lion, calf, man, and the eagle. They all had harps for singing and they held containers that were filled with the prayers of all the saints who were in heaven. They all rejoiced because of those who were redeemed.

I stood speechless and was filled with quietness as my soul processed this remarkable scene. I was thrilled as I heard the representatives of the angels and the church which were the four Living Creatures and the twenty-four Elders around the throne rejoicing. The church and the believers of all ages who were earlier seen by John as *"kings and priests"* on earth were now in heaven. It was very apparent that a translation of the people of God to heaven had taken place. They sang *"You are worthy to take the scroll, and to open its seals; for you were slain, and have redeemed us to God by your blood out of every tribe and tongue and people and nation, and have made us kings and priests to our God; and we shall reign on the earth."*

It would be impossible for just the twenty-four Elders to be from every tribe and tongue and people and nation. The church and

A Look Beyond

believers of all ages were there too, as a vast number of redeemed were singing. These redeemed were joined by thousands and thousands of angels also around the throne and they all said, *"Worthy is the Lamb who was slain to receive power and riches and wisdom, and strength and honor and glory and blessing!"*

I couldn't believe the purity and beauty of the sound. The whole of the heavens must have felt and heard what I was hearing. Then my ears were filled with what seemed to be an explosion of voices as everyone from all over heaven spoke the praises of Almighty God. One of the most amazing things about all of the rejoicing that I heard was that it came from a mixture of all of what were known as the world's languages. It was as if the languages returned to what it was like prior to the time of the Tower of Babel in the Old Testament.

I knew that all of the people represented there spoke multiple languages, but we understood all of them. It seemed as if they were speaking in their native tongue but their rejoicing was in a language that was unique to heaven, and everyone understood it. It was a powerful time that captured the innocence of a new creation in God. What rejoicing! What praise! What unity in Christ! Then I understood the scripture, *"we shall be like him; for we shall see him as he is."*

Then there was a moment that I saw for this occasion, which transpired just before the wrath of God began to be poured out on the earth. It was at this time that all creatures took part, both those who understood who God was and those who may have been indifferent to the authority of God. What happened was that *"Every creature which is in heaven, and on the earth, and under the earth, and such as are in the sea, and all that are in them, heard I saying, Blessing, and honor, and glory, and power, be unto him that sits upon the throne, and unto the Lamb for ever and ever."*

David E. Siriano

Could this be true? It's as if God took me to the end of time before the New Heaven and the New Earth were created when there would be a time in the presence of God that *"every knee shall bow to me, and every tongue shall confess to God"*. I saw those that were under the earth that were abiding in the pits of hell take the time to acknowledge their separation from God and honor His name as the righteous God even though they were lost for all of eternity.

I saw all creatures of the earth and sea that couldn't speak, and without a word being said, they seemed to rise up in joy and honor as their posture and movement gave honor and praise to God. They seemed to jump with joy and excitement in praise. It was as though all creatures were glowing with brightness. How was that possible? I did not know. One thing for sure, I was ecstatic with joy and exuberance. I couldn't hold back as I praised God with every ounce of strength that was within me! I shouted and praised and if I would still have had earthly lungs, it seems they would have exploded.

With everything that I saw, I stood trembling in the presence of God. I felt like I could have fainted, the power of that joy was so consuming. I knelt without fear but with amazement and awe! Then something happened that I least expected. I didn't realize it but God was going to ask me to do something that no one else had ever done before!

RETURN TO EARTH

As I stood there praising God I heard Him call my name, "Joseph!" I thought maybe I was imagining it but then I heard my name again, "Joseph!" I said "speak Lord." God then said, "I have an assignment for you. I want you to leave heaven and return to earth and live through the Great Tribulation." Just like that, He spoke those words, "live through the Great Tribulation." What? I couldn't believe my ears. Return to earth and leave this amazing scene and live through a time of terror that I knew was going to be seven years long? How could this be? I was stunned as I heard those words.

A feeling of sarcasm rose within me as I silently spoke to myself and said, "I knew that what I was feeling here in heaven was too good to be true!" It couldn't be that I was going to return to earth. This wasn't happening! Was everything that I believed in about heaven all of my life just a fake? Was that the voice of God I heard saying that He wanted me to go back to earth to a time that would be full of wrath and torment? Was it someone else that was saying those words and was I being tricked?

If it was God, Surely He would not send me back to the place of my old life and live the things of earth during that time! I couldn't believe it. "Yes," He said, "I want you to leave all of this and go back to earth and live through the Great Tribulation." I had just experienced the throne, the rewards, the crowns, the Judgment Seat of Christ and now God wanted me to leave I heard the voice again say, "leave!"

No! No! This was horror! I thought that once you went to heaven there was no returning to earth. Was He really asking me to go back? I thought, this must have been some sort of hallucination or even a reincarnation that I didn't even believe in. Was it a punishment that I didn't know anything about and that was never revealed in the Bible? Maybe it was because I still had sin in my life and that I carried it to heaven. How was that even possible?

Maybe there really is no hell and God was now asking me to live 'hell on earth'. This was not right. Everything I heard about heaven was that it was a permanent place of dwelling where there was no returning to the old things of earth! I felt like crying 'Help' but there was no one that could help me! God was sending me back and who was higher than God that I could appeal to? Who could bring me justice? There was no one, so I felt compelled to obey. I was upset to say the least!

David E. Siriano

I cringed as I left the sweetness of heaven and the presence of the throne. My family and friends that I encountered weren't around me. I seemed to spin around in reverse as I passed all of the flashes of light of the galaxies, stars, planets, comets, and the black holes of space once again. I found myself back on earth as I cringed in horrible anticipation as to what would now happen to me here. The contrast of seeing the throne of the God of heaven compared to this old earth in my mind was more than I could take. I was repulsed as a feeling of envy of those who were still in heaven gripped my mind. Why me?

I couldn't think of any occasion in God's Word when this happened. Surely someone stronger in spirit from the Bible such as Abraham, Joshua, David, Peter or Paul could return to earth and do a better job of living through the Great Tribulation than I could. None of them were asked to return to earth. I thought, what was my job? What was I to do? I knew that two prophets of old such as Elijah, Moses or Enoch were coming back in the End-Times but I knew that I wasn't one of them. God said He wanted me to go through the Great Tribulation but I didn't know enough about it even though I heard about it all of my life.

Now here I was, once again on earth. I couldn't believe that I was here and I found myself walking around in confusion. I needed to find a Bible! I needed to do some research to know all that was going on. I needed to find a church! But wait I thought, would there even be anyone in a church, anywhere at all? Weren't they all translated to heaven as I was? If God had asked me to return to earth surely He would lead me. I was scared!

How long was I in heaven? How long was I gone? I needed help. At least God sent me back to my old hometown. That was at least a good start. I may know someone. Could someone help me or was this going to be a lonely crushing experience? I had to find a television so I could find out what was going on in the earth. I remembered that the Great Tribulation was going to have

49

A Look Beyond

some awful things happen during that time. What were they and how could I live through them? My wife and children were in heaven and I had no one to turn to. I was all alone. Would I find people that I know or were they all gone too? I thought, please God help me! It seemed as if this was an impossible task for me to work with.

Chapter Six: The Curse Begins

I f I was going to live in the Great Tribulation then I'd better find out something about it. I'd better know what was going to happen. In my quest for a church I went to my home church first. I felt that it would be a good place to start. I went there on a Monday but the doors were locked. I asked some neighbors if they had seen anyone come into the church office that day and they said that no one did. In fact they said, no one was there yesterday either.

I thought of course, when the translation of the church took place those who were the true believers would have been taken to heaven. I found that to be true as I tried to locate people in other churches and they were not around either. However, as I searched in some churches, they still had people to fill them. I thought, how was it possible that there were people in some churches, but there were none in other churches. The people from the church I attended were gone. I thought yes, I understand.

I remember years ago preachers saying that *"one shall be taken, and the other left"*. Some were not ready to meet Christ in the translation of the church to heaven so they were left behind. Wow I thought, I remember hearing in church what Jesus said, *"But take heed to yourselves, lest your hearts be weighed down*

51

with carousing, drunkenness, and cares of this life, and that Day come on you unexpectedly. For it will come as a snare on all those who dwell on the face of the whole earth. Watch therefore, and pray always that you may be counted worthy to escape all these things that will come to pass, and to stand before the Son of Man."

That's it! As Jesus said, some would escape! Some were gone! Others were left behind. The ones left behind were part of an apostate church that met for reasons other than a believing, personal relationship with Christ. The Spirit of Christ was not living in them. They had made no commitment to serve Christ with all of their heart and they still lived in a sinful way that was not pleasing to God. They were only using church as a means of advancing their status in society.

But why did I have to come back? Was it to be a witness to these nonbelievers or was a mistake made in initially allowing me be to be taken to heaven in the first place? Was I rejected and had to return to earth? What was happening to me was difficult to swallow. I just wasn't sure. My understanding of the situation I was in was completely gone. I was begging God to give me an answer even though I was back on earth. I had a feeling of abandonment but I knew that I was going to be a witness of the coming events. I was about to see what was going to happen on earth throughout the entire tribulation.

After the church was gone there was much unrest in the world. I went to my house that we had lived in and found that things were pretty much the same except that my entire family was missing. They were in heaven. Why was I stuck here as the dilemmas of the world were ready to unfold? Would I be led of God to know exactly what I was supposed to do? How bad were things going to be and how long was I here for? I was about to see a panoramic view of the destructive events that would take place over the next seven years.

David E. Siriano

I went into a local restaurant to order a meal. Not that I was that hungry but I just had to see what others were saying. I had to find out what was going on. As I sat down I noticed on their television sets that leaders of the world, including our President, were being interviewed about some of the unusual events that had been happening. It seems that millions of people around the world were missing. They didn't know where they were or how or why they were gone. Some had suspected that aliens had come and kidnapped them to another planet. No one had any answers.

They as well as others were alarmed as they were talking about the importance of staying together in unity. Various leaders were in contact with each other and were saying that everyone should not panic but come together for peace, harmony, agreement and understanding. It seemed like a monumental task but everyone knew the importance of the decisions they were going to make.

WORLD GOVERNMENT

The leaders of the world were putting forth the idea that there needed to be a worldwide plan if peace was to be sustainable. Governments would have to work together as an international community. There had to be a way that would stop those who would capitalize on the worldwide confusion and use war and terrorism to bolster their lust for personal power. As days went by many of the powerful industrial nations of the world began to seek solutions to the quagmire that the world seemed to be engulfed in.

For some reason that I was unable to understand, the problems of the Middle East had been magnified many times over in the minds of many people. Once again, the world began to blame all of the problems of the world on the Jewish people who seemed to be in the middle of much of the leadership in big government and big business. The believing church was now in heaven so the nation of Israel was an easy target as other religions have come against them.

Persecution of the Jewish people fits in with what I heard a Pastor speaking years ago about the End-Times when he said that the Great Tribulation was originally designed for the nation of Israel long before the church began. He quoted a passage in Deuteronomy that said *"And the LORD WILL SCATTER YOU AMONG THE PEOPLES, AND YOU WILL BE LEFT FEW IN NUMBER AMONG THE NATIONS WHERE THE LORD WILL DRIVE YOU. BUT FROM THERE YOU WILL SEEK THE LORD YOUR GOD, AND YOU WILL FIND HIM IF YOU SEEK HIM WITH ALL YOUR HEART AND WITH ALL YOUR SOUL. When you are in distress, and all these things come upon you in the latter days, when you turn to the LORD YOUR GOD AND OBEY HIS VOICE (for the LORD YOUR GOD IS A MERCIFUL GOD), HE WILL NOT FORSAKE YOU NOR DESTROY YOU, NOR FORGET THE COVENANT OF YOUR FATHERS WHICH HE SWORE TO THEM."*

I thought, that is absolutely correct. The Messiahship of Christ had to be proved to the nation of Israel and not the church. The church had already believed in Jesus Christ as the Messiah and the true believers in Him were gone and now in heaven. It came to me that the Great Tribulation was for God's Covenant people, the nation of Israel. Being scattered around the world, they fulfilled the promise to Abraham that said *"in thee shall all families of the earth be blessed."* Now, their tribulation time was going to save them as a nation. I knew that the scripture said, *"Blindness in part has happened to Israel until the fullness of the Gentiles has come in. And so all Israel will be saved."*

A Psalm came to my mind that I remembered about what some nations could have in mind as far as the nation of Israel is concerned. The Psalm said, *"Come, and let us cut them off from being a nation, that the name of Israel may be remembered no more."* Will this be the beginning of horrible troubles for that tiny nation that was surrounded by so many enemies? I thought of what Jesus said, *"...the time is coming that whoever kills you will think that he offers God service."*

There was talk about the governments banding together for a peaceful solution for the troubles that everyone was facing. Some were even seeking this One-World Government with central leadership and control. Will they be concerned about the nation of Israel or will they cast it aside? The world was going through sweeping changes and momentous problems financially, militarily and politically. Crises were breaking out all over the world as rogue nations tried to make a name for themselves. Terrorism was running rampant in the world and peace was difficult to come by and Israel seems to be caught in the crossfire.

THE ANTICHRIST

World leaders were meeting but it seems that one of the leaders stood out among the rest. He had all the answers and many of the other leaders began to recognize his strength and his leadership. His words were eloquent and his mannerisms were forceful. He had a swagger about him as many seemed to trust him. He conquered nation after nation with speech and diplomacy. In some situations he came across to the nations with sharp words and threats. However, many of the nation's still put their trust in him.

He was elevated to be the leader among leaders. It was as if he was crowned above them all. Nevertheless, he still had to subdue three of the nations with war just like I remember that the prophet Daniel had predicted. He tried to force the world to change their various laws and manners of doing things. He attempted to put all things under his control. His kingdom had control over the European and Middle Eastern area. The United Nations had moved its main headquarters out of the United States and located it permanently in Geneva, Switzerland. This made it easier for him. Now the member nations of that political body were so enthralled and trusting of this powerful leader.

I recalled again in the book of Daniel that said that there would be nations in the last days that would have to submit to a leader that would be fierce and powerful. He said that some would resist him. Somehow I knew in my heart of hearts that the man who was standing out among the rest was this person. I somehow knew that he was the beast that the book of Revelation talked about who was also referred to elsewhere in the Bible as the Antichrist. He has followed a long line of Antichrists that have existed in the world for hundreds of years.

As the scriptures have predicted, *"this is that spirit of Antichrist, whereof ye have heard that it should come; and even now already is it in the world." "It is the last time: and as ye have heard that Antichrist shall come, even now are there many Antichrists; whereby we know that it is the last time."* He is the final Antichrist and the effect of his power is being felt and his authority will continue to exist throughout the entire years of the Great Tribulation. The world did not know what was ahead for them in the future.

He was able to negotiate a peace for seven years just like Daniel wrote. I remembered it was only going to be a temporary appeasement for the nations of the world. This agreement increased certain rights for the Arabs who lived in Palestine and enforced their power and statehood. It also brought about a calm to the nation of Israel as they were able to live at peace with their Arab neighbors. According to Daniel he is going to break this agreement after only three and one half years when he reveals his true evil nature. As the Bible says, *"...when they shall say, Peace and safety; then sudden destruction cometh upon them...*

Things were moving very quickly but I felt that great havoc was soon to fall on the earth. I knew that things were too unstable and that this Antichrist would declare that he is God just as I read in the Bible. I was scared but knew that my only hope was to trust in the God that I had believed in on earth and encountered in heaven, and not this man. Others trusted in him but I knew enough not to. I was praying every day for strength.

Periods of peace were hallmarks of his early time in power. However, his elevation to this position of trust that was given him only led to war. While there was some moments of peace, there was continued aggravation around the world as trust was replaced by mistrust. Schisms abounded as he tried to bring about the unity that so many longed for. He blamed the world's difficulty on the other nations of the world that weren't aligned with him. He tried to take advantage of the situation to show himself as a peacemaker in order to gain power and prominence.

The book of Revelation describes him as being on a horse. That's only symbolic because it simply means that his power and authority will move as swift as a running horse as he gains control over much of the earth. He is moving quickly as nation after nation is coming under his influence. He will use the speed of modern day weaponry to bolster his strength.

His horse is also described as being white, showing that he is a counterfeit to the Divine Christ whom the Bible says is returning to earth on a white horse at the end of the Great Tribulation. I knew that from the first time I saw this Antichrist that his power would last for the entire seven years of the agreement among the nations of the world.

WAR, FAMINE, AND DEATH

God showed me that total peace would soon be gone as wars ravaged nations in various parts of the world. These wars raced like the swiftness of a horse across the globe just like the power of the Antichrist did. Wars were moving with great speed as nations were at odds with each other as a spirit of

A Look Beyond

war gripped the world. The world leaders seemed to forget the lessons that prior generations learned who fought in WW I and WW II, as wars were once again raging throughout Europe, Northern Africa, and the Middle East. Russia has also been involved in the fray as they were sending troops into the Middle East to protect their interests there. A real spirit of hate and antagonism gripped the hearts of the armies of the world as a spirit of war seemed to loom on the horizon.

Civil war was terrorizing the Arab world as they were divided among themselves about the use of terrorism. War in the Arab world was a powerful means of demanding one's way. Factions within Islam has caused terrorism to reach an all-time high as self-destructive suicide bombers did as much damage as possible. Many thousands of people were killed in this manner all around the world as the various terrorist groups tried to gain international attention.

Of course, I knew that many of the people of the Arab world were not necessarily directly involved in the acts of terrorism. However, they were secretly and silently supportive of overcoming any way of life that was not directly linked to their belief in Islam, no matter how it was accomplished. I remembered that the Bible had said about Ishmael the father of the Arab people, that *"He shall be a wild man; His hand shall be against every man, and every man's hand against him."*

Some of the neighboring nations that were affected by all of the fighting were severely weakened while others fell apart and were divided into smaller multiple nations. Many leaders refused to talk to each other and the ones who did would only threaten one another and leave meetings or discussions with nothing accomplished. Tensions were running high as nations were threatening war on each other. Instability was commonplace and fear was gripping the hearts of the people.

The way things looked, it could only get worse and indeed I sensed that I caught a glimpse of how these wars would last for years.

Migrants were marching across all parts of the world to escape the wars and calamity. They were also marching for food as many people were desperate as famine poured in like a flood for all of the years of the Great Tribulation. They were fleeing north to France, Germany, and Sweden. Many were trying to get to the United States and Canada although travel was extremely limited because of the wars being waged across the oceans.

Some of the wealthier nations who were having shortage of foods for their own people, attempted to help the poorer nations. Food was scarce as the lands were torn with war. There was major growth in the world's population and there wasn't enough food for everyone. Mothers were desperately seeking food for their children. A great strain was placed on the world's economy and the food industry, as famine was also moving as a horse racing across the globe with speed. Famine was fast paced as it engulfed the world.

I tried to buy food with cash that I found in my pocket but was refused. A special mark was being developed for the forehead or the hand to buy daily things. I was struggling to find food myself but fortunately I had good neighbors that helped me. They were neighbors of mine when I lived here before the church was translated, but never got close to them to share the gospel with or even get to know them. We all shared what we had with each other.

These neighbors were excited to see me but wondered where my family was. When I explained how Christians were taken to heaven, their question to me was "why didn't you tell us about this so that we could have escaped the confusion that was happening now?" Now I was able to warn them as to what

A Look Beyond

was going to happen during these tribulation days. Some of them believed me because of the millions of missing people, but others weren't sure what to believe.

People were dying at an enormously fast rate. Not only were people dying because of war and famine, they were dying because of a scourge of plagues and viruses that no one was able to control. Some of it was due to animal and insect infestations. Hospitals could not keep up with the demand for doctor care and inpatient care because of the influx of patients. In some cases they were dying even before they arrived at the hospitals. Many were dying right out in the open for everyone to see. Many people never even seemed to care as they walked by the dead lying in the streets. The catastrophe was far too great for anyone to handle.

Again, like a horse racing throughout the land, death had to be dealt with for the entire years of the Great Tribulation. Death was running rampant and came quickly upon many people, whether it was in their homes, businesses, or in the streets, particularly in the larger cities around the world. All of the continents all over the world were affected not only by death everywhere but by the smell of death as well. Twenty five percent of the world's population were dying in the first years of the tribulation. The funeral directors were kept busy but they were personally struggling themselves as they had to deal with members of their own families that were dying. The world was in a pandemic state of war, famine and death!

Even though after being in heaven and now back on earth, I still felt the impact of what was taking place in heaven. My spirit was not at rest as I sensed those who were under the altar in heaven. They had sacrificed their lives for the work of God and the cause of Christ during this Great Tribulation and throughout the ages past. My spirit heard the voices of past martyrs who approached God's throne, *"And they cried with a loud voice, saying, how long, O Lord, holy and true, until you judge and avenge our blood on those who dwell on the earth?"*

The answer came back from God, *"that they should rest a little while longer, until both the number of their fellow servants and their brethren, who would be killed as they were, was completed".* As a means of satisfying them and temporarily rewarding them for now, white robes of accomplishment were given to them to wear. The answer from God helped them to remain in a state of rest until the Great Tribulation was over and future rewards would be handed out.

EARTHQUAKES

Then some great and mighty chain reaction earthquakes took place over and over again pounding the world as it seemed to teeter on its axis in preparation for the great wrath to come. Volcanoes impacted the entire globe as the ash from these occurrences left plumes of smoke not only in major cities but in the countryside as well. The sun became dark because of the smoke. The sun's rays had been blocked by a mysterious heavenly meteorite object that came between it and the earth. An icy cold gripped much of the earth.

This incident was mentioned in the Bible as something that would happen before Christ's return, *"The sun shall be turned into darkness, and the moon into blood, before the great and terrible day of the LORD come. And it shall come to pass, that whosoever shall call on the name of the LORD shall be delivered: for in mount Zion and in Jerusalem shall be deliverance, as the LORD hath said, and in the remnant whom the LORD shall call."*

The rippling earthquakes and volcanoes impacted the brilliance of the moon as it appeared to be reddish or dark in color. The stars of the heavens seemed to form meteorites at an alarming rate. Some of them passed by the earth in a close trajectory while others pounded the earth numerous times. It seemed like the mountains were moved and the islands shook to their core as the earthquakes were taking place continuously. These earthquakes happened repeatedly during the entire tribulation.

People were scared. The leaders of the nations had a hard time with their composure as they too were having difficulty keeping their emotions in check. You could tell by the looks on their faces at their daily news conferences that the hardship of the tribulation days were taking a toll on their lives. They had a sense of remorse from all of the terrible and trying times that was now tearing the world apart but they couldn't do anything about it. Their plans were falling short of what the people expected them to do.

I wasn't sure at first if they knew that these were the acts of God that were happening everywhere, but then I realized that they did. They just couldn't seem to get a grasp on who God was and what He was trying to do. They turned to their great leader the Antichrist for some help and comfort but there was little he could do.

There seemed to be a great spiritual void that was nothing like anything that had been on the earth before this time. The leaders of the world as well as all people everywhere tried to hide from the wrathful events sent by God that were taking place. Some were even wishing they would die in the powerful earthquakes. They did not want to deal with the momentous problems that everyone was facing. Things were awful! I sensed that the time of God's judgment had begun.

I recalled what the prophet Daniel said to the Jewish people and was repeated by Jesus that there would be a time of trouble *such as was not since the beginning of the world to this time, no, nor ever shall be.*" The Antichrist, war, famine, death, and earthquakes were beginning to grip the entire world during all of the tribulation period. It was simple horrible! I cried as I not only saw what was happening, I felt it too!

Chapter Seven: Sealed

Even though I didn't think that I knew enough about the book of Revelation as I should have, there were a number of things that were revealed about it to me in the Spirit. Things from the Bible that I heard in Sunday school and preachers preach about began to come back to my memory. Years ago I remember hearing someone speak about angels who held control of the winds of the earth. I also remember reading about it in Revelation where it said, *"...I saw four angels standing on the four corners of the earth, holding the four winds of the earth, that the wind should not blow on the earth, nor on the sea, nor on any tree."* In the Old Testament it says something similar where it mentions, *"...four spirits of heaven, who go out from their station before the Lord of all the earth".*

At first I couldn't understand what they had to do with anything on earth. I knew that winds could come from north, south, east or west, but could it be that angels had power over the physical elements of earth as well as spiritual things? Apparently so, because that's what began to happen. It seemed to me that these were good angels and not evil ones that were holding back some of the destruction that was soon to come because it was the wrath of God that was going to fall on the earth.

Everyone new that the ecosystem was teetering on the brink of disaster and I felt that their impact would have a devastating effect on the world. Trouble for the environment was looming in front of everyone. Soon the environment was going to be a disaster. However, it was necessary that certain ministries be set aside and begin to grow and develop that would offer salvation to people by faith in Christ as these awful times were coming. Certain servants of God had to be protected.

144,000

One of those ministries gaining prominence were Jewish servants of God who began to speak about the coming Kingdom of Christ. They became believers after Christ came for the church and you could really tell that they were sincere in their faith. I met two of them that I knew as Benjamin and Andrew who were part of 144,000 certain Jewish men from around the world that God was going to use. Neither of them were married but they were descendants of the tribe of Judah. They, and the others started traveling and preaching in churches, synagogues, and even some mosques. They spoke in open air meetings and in large arenas. Because of this great ministry, many in the world were being converted to the Judeo/Christian belief system. The Lord was about to save Israel through their preaching.

Many were being healed and many were now understanding about the coming persecution of the Jews. Both Benjamin and Andrew were from America but many of their counterparts were from other tribes of Israel who now knew about the Great Tribulation. Some of them heard Christians preaching about it before all of these awful events began to take place. They all had communicated with each other that it was now their responsibility to preach around the world. They said, "we converted Jews are the only remaining believers in Christ." They felt that they were the remnant that the Bible mentions. It was an awesome challenge for all of them.

They were talking about believing on the Christ of the New Testament. "There is coming a future time in which the coming

A Look Beyond

Messiah is going to rule on the earth," they said. It was quite a change from what you knew the Jewish belief system stood for. Benjamin and Andrew told me "there are many other Jewish believers in Christ who represented each of the twelve tribes of the old Judaist system of Israel. They are all boldly speaking the words that God gave them." They told me, "We are part of that group."

12,000 of them were from each of the twelve tribes in all corners of the globe. My guess is that the reason the number twelve was so prominent in the selection of these individuals was that twelve was the number of governmental leadership in the Bible. There were twelve judges, twelve tribes, and twelve apostles. In this case in the time of the tribulation there were 12,000 from each of the twelve tribes forming a spiritual leadership of witnessing for Christ and of His coming Kingdom on earth.

All of these tribes held conferences together, discussing their ministry and how to allow God to lead them. They were crisscrossing in their travels and meeting with each other in many nations around the world throughout the year. They were not only traveling throughout the stronghold of Christianity in the continents of North and South America, they were reaching out to the cold and staid continent of Europe. Their preaching also reached the continents of Asia and Africa as many Hindus and Muslims were coming to Christ as well.

Their traveling and ministry were making a great impact as they were moving around the globe by air, train, bus, and automobile. By any means that they could, they were spreading their message boldly and affectively. Some were traveling to remote areas by horseback, motorcycle and boat. Their ministry was gaining great momentum as nothing could hold them back. It reminded me of the days of the Apostle Paul and his missionary journeys in the Bible.

David E. Siriano

They knew that they had a commitment to spread the gospel of Christ and His Kingdom world-wide. With the 144,000 preaching the gospel, it seems like they will be around for a long time because no one seems to be able to come against them. They would slip away from authorities every time as they could not be caught. They appear to have some kind of protective strength that keeps them safe from harm as if they were sealed by an angel that came from God. None of the evil that would come against them was able to prevent them from continuing their message. They were stirring the gospel message in the hearts of all they came in contact with.

Many people were coming to believe on Jesus Christ even though the Antichrist has been playing a major evil role in the world. He was doing his best to prevent many from believing what they were saying. He couldn't stop the 144,000 and neither could he kill them because they were that well protected. These witnesses for Jesus Christ were responsible for a large number of people coming to Christ despite the anti-Semitism that was so prevalent.

It was difficult to calculate how many were being saved because it was taking place all over the world. No one could keep up with the number of people that were coming to Christ because it was happening so fast. Even though the church was translated out of the world, millions who were left on the earth were becoming believers. And even though I wish that I was in heaven and not back here on earth, it was a strong spiritual experience for me to witness. It was amazing!

The completed Jews who were now serving Christ because of the work of the 144,000, were being persecuted not only by the Antichrist but by the apostate church that was left on the earth. They were both working in tandem to try and stop any message that they considered to be working against their political and religious agenda. While they were doing their best to stand in their way, God was developing a powerful remnant of believers world-wide. It was an amazing movement in the early part of the Great Tribulation.

These new believers were also preaching the salvation of the Lord. Those who were being saved were both Jewish people and Gentiles. While God was protecting the 144,000, many of the others who were witnessing were being killed for their faith. Some were losing their lives because of the wars, the treachery, and the persecutions that were breaking out. It was awful as they along with so many others were being caught in the crossfire of house to house combat that was taking place, and from the barbaric slaughter in diabolical plots against them.

Many of those new believers who were boldly speaking out about the Lord were being thrown in jail. Some were being openly shot in the streets or had to face a firing squad. Others were being beheaded because of their outspoken ministry. Still, nothing could hold the vast majority of them back from speaking about the God of heaven and the Lamb of God that brings salvation to the world. The impact of their ministry was immense.

One such witness who was brought to Christ by the 144,000 was a woman named Helen whom I saw being interviewed on television. She and her family came to the Lord in America but came under immediate persecution for her faith by those who were followers of the Antichrist. America was severely divided because it had gone far from the early revivals that came to America during its founding. America had changed from that earlier time. Attacks were being leveled against those who were trying to spread the gospel. She was a university professor and the government, as well as the agnostic and atheistic teachers she was associated with, made Helen pay a severe price for her witnessing.

Her husband Frank was killed in a revenge murder because she wouldn't renounce her testimony. To intimidate her further, her two teenagers were kidnapped and within three weeks their bodies were found. She found out that they too were murdered. She was being threatened as she barely escaped with her life. She sobbed repeatedly "my children, my children." She cried out "my God, why has this happened. I don't understand. Couldn't you have spared my children during this awful time?"

She could only be comforted by friends that she knew and that she fellowshipped with. They hid her but she had to move from house to house among Christian friends who were not exposed yet and were sympathetic to her cause. Though she struggled with everything that happened, she mentally relied on the fact that one day she would see her husband and children in heaven. Stories like this were being repeated around the world as many gave their lives for the sake of Christ and His word.

UNNUMBERED MULTITUDE

I saw how big and important their ministry was when all of a sudden the Spirit took me back to heaven. I was going back to heaven? Could this be happening to me again? I was not returning to heaven in my physical body but in my spiritual state of mind in a vision. I felt that God wanted me to see something that was very important. I was immediately shown a large number of people who were rejoicing victoriously. I didn't know who they were.

I began to ask anyone who would listen to me. "Who were they," I asked? I went from person to person where I was standing in the area of the Throne of God but no one would answer me. As I got closer to them I heard what they were saying, *"Salvation belongs to our God who sits on the throne, and to the Lamb!"* All of the angels of God around His throne fell before Him and worshipped Him.

A Look Beyond

That's when the Lord showed me that *"These are the ones who come out of the great tribulation, and washed their robes and made them white in the blood of the Lamb. Therefore they are before the throne of God, and serve Him day and night in His temple. And He who sits on the throne will dwell among them. They shall neither hunger anymore nor thirst anymore; the sun shall not strike them, nor any heat; for the Lamb who is in the midst of the throne will shepherd them and lead them to living fountains of waters. And God will wipe away every tear from their eyes."*

The Lord had taken me seven years into the future after the Great Tribulation was over, to visualize their place in heaven. I saw a large multitude of people that no one could number who had overcome the horribleness of that time of terror and were now safe in the presence of God. I was astounded as I saw the end result of all their labors and trials! Many of them were killed for their faith. I was deeply moved as I realized how sweeping and powerful the ministry of the 144,000 was.

I saw Helen's husband Frank and their children who were martyred. I had seen pictures of them on television so I knew that they were safe. They were rejoicing in the presence of the Lord. I tried to find out how many others were there around the throne and who had come out of the Great Tribulation through martyrdom but it seemed no one could satisfy my inquiry. Those who were martyred were too vast to number.

In this experience that God gave me, there they were, worshipping God with loud words and songs of praise for all of the victories that God gave them. I was shaken in my spirit as I viewed this glorious scene. It was beautiful. God was on His throne and He was exalted before His subjects! I just felt that I needed to bow before the throne again in thankfulness. I was thrilled to be able to see these Jewish witnesses and their Gentile counterparts now enjoying the blessings and benefits of serving Christ for eternity. Their witnessing was over.

Their struggle to maintain their lives and dignity was rewarded. There was no more suffering for them as they were now enjoying their eternal state of being. They were praising God and exalting His Holy Name as all of heaven had welcomed them home. The earlier announcement that the martyrs whose spirits were already in heaven had to wait until more martyrs were killed, was now complete.

Chapter Eight: Herald the Trumpets

Although I recognized that I was on earth in my hometown, I continued to see visions in my spirit that I could hardly believe. All of the rejoicing in heaven that seemed to be going on endlessly, suddenly come to an abrupt halt as a deafening silence prevailed and permeated the entire heavens and the throne room of God as well. I heard no voices! No one was speaking! No one was singing! No one was rejoicing! Wow, I thought. What was the problem? Did the individuals in heaven who were praising God suddenly grow weary? Did they need a rest? Were they going to concentrate on something else? What was going on? I did not know why there was this quiet in heaven.

Everyone stood in absolute silence. I couldn't believe it! The angels stood still. Their wings did not move at all. The four living creatures were motionless. The twenty-four Elders offered no praise. The millions upon millions of the people of God who had been rejoicing endlessly were like statues. It seemed like the heavens themselves came to a grinding halt. This hush became an agonizing expectancy as if something terrible was about to happen. The seconds of silence turned into minutes. The minutes were painfully long. A half hour went by. What was about to happen? It was as if God Himself had nothing to say or do. How could this be?

The answer to my questions came immediately. The thirty minutes of breathless silence in heaven tore at the hearts of everyone who was standing there with nothing to say. It was as if they knew what was about to happen. God was ready to unleash the fury that seemed to have been pent up within Him for thousands of years. He was a merciful and patient God who was awaiting repentance from His creation but to no avail. What was about to happen was going to be the beginning of His claims to the earth and the universe that all of creation belonged to Him. This claim was in the proof of His power. Only He could exercise this kind of vengeance. The wrath to reclaim what was His was about to begin. Time had run out. I thought "Oh God, please, help us all!"

PRAYERS OF GOD'S PEOPLE

What happened next while in the spirit was almost unbelievable. I saw an angel take a golden container with a fiery smoke-filled aroma that was mixed with the prayers of the saints and offer it up to God as lights for Him to see. The light of their prayers seemed to break through from the earth below to the heavens above. It pierced the most difficult and hardened principalities and powers that were attempting to block its path. These prayer-filled shafts of light reached the heart of God. They were from the believers living in the Great Tribulation, and from the thousands of years of prayers offered by the people of God who were now standing in front of God Himself.

These prayers were now calling on God to impose strong retribution for all of the years of a creation that was unrepentant. It was just like when I saw the saints crying under the altar moments before because of their martyrdom and their blood being spilled on the earth. Because of the many injustices of the past, God had to take action. God was ready to bring closure for Israel and all of the people of God on earth.

A Look Beyond

These prayers of theirs were mixed with the incense that was the angel's responsibility to show and remind God of the wrath that was necessary for Him to unleash. That mixture of prayers along with fire that the angel took from the altar of God became a startling picture of the wrath of God as the angel cast the fiery smoke filled prayers to the earth. The prayers of God's people became a part of the wrath that was poured out upon the earth. The heavens were filled with voices, and thunder, and lightning, and an earthquake. The earthquake hit the earth with great devastation. God's people with their prayers were calling for vengeance from God that He would pour His wrath upon the earth. It was startling and powerful! I was scared for the earth as I felt that the severe judgment of God was about to begin.

SEVEN ANGELS

Seven angels were then dispatched to blow trumpets in the form of announcements of doom and destruction. I was trembling in my spirit but I knew what was about to happen because my body was still on earth. My family was OK because they were in heaven, but what about me? What was I about to endure? Again I cried out, "please God, help me and lead me." I was literally shaking with fear as I expected the worse here on earth.

I knew that the awful events of the End-Times were going to take a horrible and drastic turn. Things were ramping up in the world as the one man whom I suspected as the Antichrist was gaining more power. But those angels! I saw them streaking across the sky, flying first across land and then over the oceans as if to make plans in what they were getting ready to do. I'm not sure if anyone else saw them but they were preparing to allow tragic events to happen on the earth with their announcement trumpets.

This is about the time that I met Markell. We met when I got a job at a local manufacturing plant as I tried to support myself in the midst of all the fear and financial problems we were all facing. I looked for a job in my profession as a teacher but schools used what few teachers they had contracts with, while other schools were closed as many teachers and younger children were missing. The problems for the school districts were immense. Markell was a congenial guy, young and well liked. He seemed to have a good head on his shoulders. I didn't know him for very long but I got some first-hand information from him about the devastation that was happening to his family in Europe. He had some relatives and friends that were living in Germany where he was originally from. He and I were having some long talks about the trouble that all of the world was facing. We saw a lot of it on television and we also witnessed disturbing local events as well.

The worst of it for Markell was concerning his mother and father back in Germany. He was in contact with them as best he could on a daily basis by phone, but satellite service was weak because of much of the destruction that was happening around the world. Many powerful leaders were vying for power in Europe and the Middle East and he was concerned for his family there. They were contending with each other because some were supportive of the new world leader and some were not.

His parents were retired and were struggling to make ends meet. He told me, "they had their own garden but it was becoming increasingly difficult to acquire what was necessary to sustain themselves." He found out that his brothers and sisters had fled to Switzerland where the United Nations was, thinking that they could escape the horror that was happening in the rest of Europe. They soon realized that neutral Switzerland was not safe anymore either as the persecution and calamities of the world had affected that country as well.

That beautiful country was being stripped of its fine culture and beautiful art. Its magnificent homes and mountain ranges they overlooked were being ruined. Fires were raging out of control and were ruining the countryside. Markell told me these reports

A Look Beyond

and we saw them on television and the internet. We both thought, this was it! It was all over for mankind. Hell was about to be unleashed on earth. He said, "I haven't found out what happened to all of my family but I am hoping for the best."

All of that was beginning to happen as the first angel came from heaven and sounded his trumpet and the earth was bombarded with hail and fire mixed with blood. This mixture of terror fell to the earth in similar fashion as the plagues in Egypt during the days of Moses. The hail were huge ice balls that were mixed with fire, giving the appearance of blood as it created fires all over the world. Businesses and homes were burning in all sections of the world. Cities, small villages, and towns were being destroyed.

The hail had instigated mini-wars and large scale wars in all corners of the globe as nations thought that other nations were attacking them. The great leader that was elevated by the many nations of the world who at first came in peace was now conducting campaigns of war to further his insatiable desire for control. War was flaming in the continents of the Far East, Middle East, Europe, Northern Africa and the Americas. Everything was out of control.

Fires were breaking out from the angel that cast fire to the earth and also from the wars that engulfed cities like New York, Chicago, Los Angeles, Paris, Moscow, Tokyo, and Beijing as nations fired powerful weapons at each other. Fighting, bombing, gang wars and shootings were common on the streets and in schools and universities. With people in a state of panic, riots were common place. Terrorism continued with mass shootings almost every day in malls, sports gatherings, businesses, restaurants and other public places. These evil people who committed these atrocities were copying the evil deeds of others as things got out of hand. Some people were afraid to venture out into the public. Many were angry and blaming all of the catastrophes on God.

David E. Siriano

One third of trees were burning and all grass in the world burned on every continent. Fields turned desert-like and couldn't grow food. Crops and plant life seemed to be singled out and destroyed. They burned as wildfires ensued from the conflagrations of fires and wars. I recalled the fires in California and in the west in years past and they were nothing compared to the fires that now raged out of control. All of us here on earth were running and trying to hide from the out of control fires and war. I have to admit things were so bad, I was scared and running for my life.

Then more horribleness came at the sound of the second angel as it seemed like great fiery mountains were falling and burning in the sea as it incited war to start across the vast waters. Hundreds of thousands of battleships and submarines had gathered in the oceans around the world and were firing volleys of cannon shots, torpedoes and depth charges at each other as warfare increased exponentially. Small scale nuclear and chemical weapons were being fired in most of the oceanic waters. They were rising out of the waters rearing themselves up like volcanic surges of fire in the oceans. One third of battleships and submarines were destroyed. Planes were being shot out of the sky.

The fires were disbursed and there appeared the blood of millions of ocean creatures as one third of them died all over the earth because of the wars and fires. One third of the ocean waters were filled with blood because of the disasters. The warheads became torrents of choking smoke that filled the skies from one hemisphere to another. We were all struggling to breathe. Wars involving these weapons raged across the nations causing chemical reactions in the seas in every hemisphere. Men who had evacuated ships came in contact with the chemicals in the waters and died when it was absorbed into their skin. Besides the naval ships, other ships were destroyed as they attempted to cross the ocean waters.

A Look Beyond

All of this had a major impact on the industries of all of the nations as trade and productivity was scaled back to practically zero. The days seemed to never end, as day after day, everyone waited for nightfall with the hope that things would calm down. It seemed to me that World War Three was on the horizon and I did not want to get caught in the middle of it.

Computer launched cyber-attacks from some nations against other nations became a part of growing threats against international security and defense systems around the world. I was scared knowing that another angel was about to appear. What could happen next? What was the next catastrophe?

Then the third angel's trumpet announcement came and my greatest fear came over me. Something fiery fell from the sky and I knew it hit America. At first I wasn't sure if it was a meteorite or a nuclear weapon. I panicked as I looked at the internet on my phone and I saw a series of other similar fires falling from the sky all over the world.

I then realized that nations were now using super guns and also firing nuclear weapons at each other as well as what the angel cast to the earth. Many were losing their lives in the countries where they were lobbing these weapons. People were dying in the streets as their flesh disintegrated. It seemed like hundreds of these fiery weapons were being poured out of the upper atmosphere. I remember the Gulf War, and just as bombs were launched with precision into buildings then, so too that is what was happening now. Neutron bombs were also being used causing extensive loss of life but relatively little damage to buildings and property. Cities that were once filled with activity were now void of life as wars continued to increase.

These weapons hit the inland parts of each of the continents. They were polluting almost everything in sight, especially lakes and rivers that supplied the drinking water on the earth. People were dying of thirst. In America, the rivers that were hit particularly hard were the Colorado, Missouri, Mississippi, and Ohio rivers. Most people would hesitate when they went to drink but there were many who drank the water anyway. They died almost immediately. Even all around the world, everyone was looking for water to drink, and when possible some were driving for miles just to satisfy their thirst. One third of the waters became toxin and bitter to the taste. It was awful.

It seemed like all of the destructive fires unleashed by the angels were overlapping each other so that before one ended another one came. It was getting worse as wave after wave of fiery destruction and turmoil were destroying the earth and waters. I was trying to recover from difficulty breathing, running from the previous angelic calamitous fires that were being unleashed. I was going everywhere that I could think of, just to look for water.

Then the fourth angel sounded his trumpet. What happened next was too much to bear. I knew that I needed to find a place to hide. All of the smoke and toxic air from the fires, the volcanos, and the nuclear weapons continued to darken the sun, moon, and stars day after day. The sun being darkened happened repeatedly. One third of the day became as night as the sun's rays from the heavens seemed to diminish. The moon appeared to have vanished and you could barely see the stars anymore. Everything in the heavens have changed dramatically. The universe was reeling out of control.

The pain and death from this punishment was too heartbreaking and harmful. Everyone was scared and it was still difficult to breathe. A fierce panic had settled into the populations of the world. Even the leaders of the nations had no answers to calm the fear of the people. God was allowing the will of evil to have its way. It was truly what the Bible predicted, *"Men's hearts failing them for fear, and for looking after those things which are coming on the earth: for the powers of heaven shall be shaken."*

A Look Beyond

I was struggling with the assignment from God that I had to live through the Great Tribulation. I saw the pain and despair. I heard the cries not only at night but also during the day. They did not quit. I was struggling myself just to keep up with the daily rigors of life. I remembered back when some Christians thought they were living through the tribulation then. I now knew that this was tribulation! The pain, the difficulty and the wrath of God was falling on the earth. It was more than many could bear and more then what I felt I could pass through without help. Oh, how I wish that my wife was here so she could comfort me. But then I thought, no! She and the children are better off in heaven. I would not wish what I am going through on anyone. Lord, please help us at this moment!

WOE, WOE, WOE

Then there was a sound that I'm not sure anyone else heard. An angel was flying in the sky and screaming at the top of his voice saying that the last three angelic trumpet judgments of the seven would be more horrible than the first four. The last three angels were ready to come. No, how could this be? How can things get any worse? I was alarmed as I heard the angel cry out in rapid succession, 'Woe, Woe, Woe', signifying the horribleness of what was about to happen with the next three angels. He was saying it over and over again. I could only imagine that he was flying all around the world with these three words of the coming devastation.

I'm not sure if everyone could hear this angel but they must have. It surely was going to affect their daily life and the lives of everyone else on the planet. I knew that the entire world would be turned upside down and nobody could do anything about it. I do know this, all of the world's leaders and everyone else felt hopeless as they were all at a loss. The impact of the angel's message was for all the world to know. The world was beginning to reel with pain as the environment was changing right before everyone's eyes. No one could have predicted this and nobody could stop it. Industry and trade were severely impacted.

The world was seeking to find solutions on their own. The nations would not turn to God for help. There was no sorrow and no repentance. The world continued in its evil ways. The leaders of the nations continued to pass laws against God's word. Therefore, God's plan of wrath was in place. Would the pain never end? Was there any hope? I wasn't sure. My spirit welled up within me as I cried out in this horrible tribulation, "Please God, help me and save me from this destruction!"

Chapter Nine: Devastation

Then the fifth angel came which had the first woe. On earth I looked up to the sky and believe it or not, I saw a spirit-like individual descend from heaven like a falling star. I knew in my spirit that he had been given the key and authority over what looked like to me in a vision as a pit with no bottom. There was no end to it. I wasn't positive if this individual was the Devil, one of his agents, or even if it was an angel from God, but he opened it. All kinds of grief and calamity were released upon the world with this first woe!

This bottomless pit was a place of endless existence that was filled with darkness, emptiness and nothingness and I surely didn't want to get near it. I wasn't sure where it was located and I don't know how I knew it but it was either in the earth or somewhere like a black hole in space that nothing could escape from. The key that this individual had been given, gave him the knowledge as to how to open it for evil to escape.

He allowed a horrible dark smoke to come upon the earth from the darkness of that pit that had a foul smell of death. It was as if darkness was able to escape from darkness. The dark smoke that came from the pit obscured the sun, clogged the air and pervaded the entire world. Everyone had a hard time seeing. Many people couldn't leave their house, and they couldn't drive. The best they could do was stay at home and keep the windows closed so that they would not be bothered by the heavy dark smoke. It was demonic!

This pit was known by the demons during the days of Jesus because on one occasion when He went to cast out a legion of spirits from an individual, they didn't want to go into the deep, or in other words the pit. I'm not sure, but many spirits must have been roaming in and out of this pit as I saw it. It was the worst feeling that I could have ever had.

DEMONIC INVASION

Once the smoke was in the air, out of it came terrible, frightening multi-headed demonic looking creatures. They didn't look like they were living creatures, but mechanical. I asked some people that I had just met, Charles and Barbara, if they had seen them because they were as real to me as anything else. They answered, "No we hadn't seen them." I was shocked. Was the smoke so dense that they could not be seen? Was I the only one that knew that they were there? Was I the only one that detected them? It could have been that my spiritual eyes had been opened after being in heaven and others were blind to what was happening. I don't know, but what I saw was awful. To me, this was the worst part of what I was experiencing.

They were devilish inspired and they swarmed the earth as warfare began to be waged everywhere. Nation was rising against nation as destruction became world-wide. These horrible monsters were numerous like locusts. They really weren't locusts because they didn't harm the vegetation. Also, they had a leader, but I remembered that the Bible says that locusts don't need a leader. They were something other than locusts. They were frightening!

They were there to bring harm to anyone who wasn't protected by God. That meant a lot of people were tormented by these

A Look Beyond

hellish mechanical creatures with harmful stings and burns that would eat their flesh alive. Pieces of their flesh would fall off by just simply touching it. They were tortured beyond imagination for months as some of the stings and burns also developed into diseases that turned into sores and viruses. Many of those who were tormented wanted to die but they could not find death.

Charles and Barbara were running for their lives. Everyone ran to friends' homes, hospitals and the places where they worked but they could not find help or comfort. Their faces were distorted beyond recognition. When their skin would fall off, it would only grow back and then fall off again. Their torment was unbearable. I was running and dodging all of the fire power, but these creatures missed and did not harm me and I didn't know why. I certainly wasn't a part of the 144,000 that were protected and I didn't have any other means of protection. For some reason I wasn't struck by their power that could hit me and inflict pain. I was thankful!

With all of the suffering, I then realized that everyone was seeing these horrible creatures and not just me. They were plentiful and moving in warfare all over the world. Everyone was running away from them but there was no place to hide. People saw them swarming all over the earth. They were all running scared like animals in packs and groups. They went from house to house in fear. They were running or got in their vehicles but had no place to hide.

Public transportation such as planes, buses, trains, or even a taxi were not available because those who would fly or drive them were suffering just like everyone else. Places of work, office buildings, banks and local, state and federal government buildings were closed because of the pain and panic. It caused unbelievable fear because many people couldn't work or even get a ride to work. Some ran to the mountains in fear.

David E. Siriano

The description of these creatures were horrifying. John described them in the book of Revelation as best he could with the language of his day. I'm sure he had never seen anything like them in his life. He would have had no idea what to describe or give names to what he saw. I remembered what he said about these awful creatures. They moved as swift as horses across the countryside. They were ferocious and ready for battle.

Out of that putrid dark smoke came swooping unmanned drone-like flying machines propelled with great speed, as well as powerful jets that raced swiftly across the sky. They must have been sent by the warring nations that were fighting with each other. They flew across the sky with incredible precision and force. People were running from house to house to escape the rocket fire and machine gun fire that seemed to be everywhere. I was in a state of panic as I experienced the closeness of war. I was still trying to avoid the weapons that were flying all around me. My life was hanging in the balance every day. I was trying to find friends that I knew that could help shelter me. It was a day by day struggle just to find food and housing.

Newspapers were difficult to come by but I read that the nations of the east were sending their helicopters and jets to fight the nations in Europe. Drones were being launched from military placements throughout Europe and Asia as these two great continents were once again at war with each other. Large cities like Tokyo, Shanghai, Moscow, London, and Paris were caught in the middle of the battles. We here in North and South America could not escape the carnage of these destructive airborne vehicles as cities such as Mexico City, Toronto, San Francisco, Houston and Philadelphia were right in the crossfire of the fires and destruction.

Everyone described the drones as controlling, locust-like creatures with crowns on their heads that appeared to be motors. Around the entire drones were the fronts of what looked like faces of men that were menacing and hateful, leading the way to destruction. There were many thousands of these weapons that were destroying people and property. They were military-like devils that were difficult to fight against as thousands were dying in the city streets and in the country sides.

Fire and smoke came trailing out of the backs of the jets like contrails of condensed vapors. The smoke gave them the appearance of having the glory and tenderness of flowing women's hair, but they were really evil and cruel. Their front fire power similar to guns propelling lasers, looked like the teeth of lions in a heightened strength of destruction. Their protective breastplates were the armor of iron and steel that helped keep them safe from enemy fire. The wing-like rotor blades of the helicopters helped them fly swiftly, making powerful military type noises with their engines. Their tails were also full of stinging, scorpion-like artillery fire power that caused as much death and destruction as possible. It was modern-day warfare at its worst as nations were reeling in horror and destruction.

Their leader, who was called a king in John's day, came from the bottomless pit and was directing the unmanned drones with a controlling unmanned mothership. He was like the right hand man of Satan that lured the demonic spirit-like weaponry into action that had influence over the war-torn world and the military might that came from the nations. The name of that leader was 'destruction'. All of these mechanical creatures made a mess of the world. The entire human creation of God was now being unbelievably transformed and tormented. There didn't seem to be any hope in sight as this ended the first woe. Thank God it was over.

200 MILLION SOLDIERS

Then came the sixth angel that had the second woe. What should I expect next? I didn't know. As I was praying about what was going to happen, I sensed that this angel was told to free the four angels that were bound at the river Euphrates that flowed through Turkey, Syria, and Iraq. This command came from the golden altar that was in heaven. Because it came from God I felt that it had to be important and I thought the worst was about to happen. Good angels are not bound so I figured that they had to be evil angels that were being freed for this particular day and year. Once again, I was frightened. What was going to happen?

When I went back home I saw on television the armies of millions of soldiers coming mostly from Asia but from other parts of the world as well. It was as if they were preparing for some big event that was to take place soon. Some of the newsmakers were estimating that the armies were numbered at over two hundred million men and women who were ready for battle. Soldiers walked, rode in jeeps, tanks, all-terrain vehicles, mine resistant vehicles, and flew in jets and helicopters. There were unmanned ground drone fighting machines that were part of this massive army that terrorized the world with their powerful fire power. All of them were very agile and moved with great speed.

These vehicles propelled grenades and explosive devises that created havoc throughout Asia as they marched westward toward the Middle East. They were creating war and terrorism where ever they went. There was fighting in China, India, Pakistan, Afghanistan, Iran, Iraq, Turkey, Saudi Arabia, and in parts of Europe as well. Not only were army men killed, but innocent people were lying dead in the streets as this large military moved across the nations.

Their armored vehicles projected black, orange, and red fire power. Part of the army used jet and helicopter power as their guns roared with fire from the front, sides and rear, killing and maiming millions. They were swift like horses and their motorized sound was like lions that roared in their strength. Wars were again moving all over the earth. One third of those

A Look Beyond

who fought for them and against them were killed. The way things looked I could only think that many more would be killed throughout the Great Tribulation.

The saddest thing about this event and all of the events of the entire tribulation is that those who were still alive did not repent of all of the evil of murder, adultery, thievery, and drugs that they were habitually part of in the world. They did not ask for the mercy of God to fall on the earth. The leaders of the nations wanted nothing to do with God. To me it was a sad day.

I remembered the scripture in Revelation that said, *And the rest of the men which were not killed by these plagues yet repented not of the works of their hands, that they should not worship devils, and idols of gold, and silver, and brass, and stone, and of wood: which neither can see, nor hear, nor walk: Neither repented they of their murders, nor of their sorceries, nor of their fornication, nor of their thefts.*

Chapter Ten: The Land and the Sea

O n earth I looked skyward, wondering if God was going to reveal any more things to me. My mind and thoughts were racing as I tried to remember my wonderful times in heaven. I missed seeing the angels of God and the Elders that were leading all of the people in praise and worship to God. As I was thinking about what I was missing, all of a sudden with my spiritual understanding, I saw another mighty angel come down from the heavens. Was this just an allusion or was I really seeing Him. He must have come from the throne room of God. What a powerful being he was and the sight of him caused me to tremble. I wondered if anyone else had seen him. Was he being revealed to the whole earth or was this something that was only being shown to me? Why was he coming down to earth and what was he going to do?

He was surrounded with clouds and a rainbow. I guess the clouds and rainbow were trying to show me the heavenly significance of his appearance. He was almost too brilliant for me to look at. He was as bright as the sun, as if the glory of God was reflecting off of his face. His feet were burning with fire. One foot was on the land and the other one was on the ocean. To me it meant that he had power and authority over both land and sea. I was struck with this amazing vision that God was revealing to me. What did it all mean?

I felt the heat from his spirit-like bodily presence. I could almost reach out and touch him although his influence was all over the world and too far away for me to reach. He had a small book in his hand and I think it was a book that contained more of the judgments of God. He looked very strong as if he was on a mission and no one could deter him from what he was about to do.

SEVEN THUNDERS

He roared with a loud voice and all of a sudden seven thunders began to roar. I suppose that if other people didn't see him they might have thought that it was a powerful storm of some kind. I know that everyone could hear the thunder because many people began to look toward the sky. There were loud thunderclaps over and over again that put a fright in my heart. Many people looked like they were confused. They ran for shelter anywhere they could find it. I did the same as the thunders began to roar louder than when they first began. I did feel at peace however because I felt sure that the angel came from God.

I began to pray again as I put my trust in God, but others were afraid. I don't think they saw the angel. Apparently the book in his hand was connected somehow to the thundering. I remember reading in the book of Revelation that the Apostle John was told not to write what they were announcing. Somehow John knew something about what was in the mind of God but he wasn't allowed to reveal it. He was prohibited from writing what they were. I don't know why he wasn't allowed to do so. My guess is that he had to conceal them because of how solemn and frightful they must have been. I felt that they were preludes to the horrible judgments that I knew were yet to come.

David E. Siriano

I didn't know what the thunder judgments were or what they meant but I felt that they were going to be awful. I had already seen thunder that was around the throne of God and that came out of the throne. Now there were repeated amounts of thunder that roared louder than any noise that could be imagined. Lightning accompanied the thunder that flashed across the sky as far as the eye could see. The whole earth must have been filled with the noise of the thunder and the flashes of lightning.

All of us were holding our ears from the deafening noise and covering our eyes from the blinding lightning. The entire sky was lit up from one end of heaven to the other. It was awful as no one seemed to be able to get any rest because of these torturous seven thunders and lightning. Day and night, the mental and emotional strain was more than any of us could bear. My only hope was that these thunders were going to complete the judgments of God. I couldn't stand it anymore. I cried to God again, "God, why did you send me back to earth? This is more than I can possibly live through. I am not sleeping and not getting any rest. Please God, help me, please."

I cringed when I thought of how powerful this revelation was to John and how catastrophic it was for me to see it happening to all of us on the earth. I saw what the thunders were but I don't know how to explain them other than what I saw. I saw them because they were happening right in front of me but they were so horrible that it was difficult to describe them in words. These thunders roaring across the sky were more powerful than anyone of us could believe.

Heaven seemed to be splitting apart as if it was crying in distress like words being spoken in sorrow. My conscious state didn't understand the words and I didn't know how to interpret them. All I know was that the universe was rumbling under the weighty words of the power of God. Something was stirring and changing in the entire universe that was a part of God's mighty wrath but

I didn't know exactly what it was. The thunders were revealed to John and he wasn't allowed to write them. I saw the thunders but I didn't know how to explain them. What a dilemma for me and my understanding. God help the world! Was it possible that I could go through anything more?

These horrendous acts of judgments from God must have been a prelude to ready the world for what I suspected were the final seven last plagues that I knew were coming from teachings I heard years ago. I remembered the scripture in Romans where it says that "*...the creation itself also will be delivered from the bondage of corruption into the glorious liberty of the children of God. For we know that the whole creation groans and labors with birth pangs together until now.*" I just felt that through this angel, God was ready to deliver the earth to its fullness. God was about to reclaim the ownership of the earth that rightfully belonged to Him. Was I right and was this what was happening? I felt that I was soon to find out. This angel lifted his hand to heaven as an oath, as if to signal that God's wrath was about to be poured out upon the earth and it was going to happen quickly.

NO MORE TIME

The angel began to stress the fact that time was running out. The seal judgments of God had already began to take place and six of the seven angels with trumpets had already announced the judgments of God. I felt that soon the seventh angel was going to sound his trumpet announcing the third woe. Time was running out. There would be no more delay in the punishment from God. Now the mighty angel that stood on the land and sea said *that "in the days of the voice of the seventh angel, when he shall begin to sound, the mystery of God should be finished".* I knew that the seventh angel was ready to make his sound. How much worse was it going to get? How much pressure can the world endure? Would things really be over?

All of a sudden my mind took me back to when the Apostle John wrote the book of Revelation. I heard a voice coming out of heaven and telling John to take the book out of the angel's hand and eat it. Eat it? I thought, it would be impossible to eat a book. Nevertheless, John went to the angel and asked for the book that he was holding. He took the book out of his hand and then I understood. It was a figure of speech. He was to eat the book in a manner of speaking. What he really was to do was absorb the words of the book into his heart and mind. He was to thoroughly digest the predictions and then speak about them again, bringing about the final move of the wrath of God. I knew that without a shadow of doubt, time was coming to an end.

At first John felt good about understanding the words of the book. He liked what he read. The words were at first sweet in his mouth but in his stomach they were awfully bitter words. He was told that he, *"must prophesy again before many peoples, and nations, and tongues, and kings."* A similar thing was asked of the Prophets Ezekiel and Jeremiah. They were told to eat the writings that God gave them. They both spoke to the house of Israel during the time of their captivity. Now I understood John's mission as he wrote the book of Revelation. What he heard and then proceeded to swallow was a message to Israel and the world. It was a message of judgment and salvation. It was happening right in front of my eyes. I saw myself as visibly shaken and literally astounded.

Chapter Eleven: Engaging the End

I began to see progress on an event that had been going on for about three years now. It has been on all of the news programs and channels. It was the plans for the building of a new Temple for the Jewish people in the city of Jerusalem. There hasn't been any work on the building of a Temple in Jerusalem for thousands of years. The Antichrist was involved as he helped bring about an agreement between the Arab and Jewish peoples in Palestine.

About three and a half years ago he helped broker a seven year peace agreement for the Middle East. It included international recognition of Jerusalem as the capital of Israel, a Temple for the Jewish people, as well as land and statehood for the Arab people. Although he did it for political reasons, everyone else was elated as the world thought that he was a genius to bring about a peace plan that everyone seemed to be satisfied with. There was rejoicing in the streets of Jerusalem for Christians, Jews and Muslims as it looked like finally, a peace will hold. All three of those religions shared the city and they were all holding their collective breath hoping for stability in unstable times.

The new Temple of God was being built right next to the Islamic Mosque of Omar. Its measurements were laid out specifically to include the altar area and all of its worshippers. The courtyard outside the temple was in control of the Gentiles as they were

David E. Siriano

in command of the city of Jerusalem for three and a half years during the second half of the tribulation.

A man by the name of Samuel that I saw being interviewed on the news, was one of the chief supervisors of the work. He has been heading up the workmen that have been preparing for the Temple. They had worked for months on the foundation. I remember seeing the beginnings of it even before the tribulation started. Their work was very diligent and with all of the pride in building it, it didn't take long for the walls to be erected. For years, they have been preparing much of the material in other parts of Israel and in other nations. Much of the furniture was being prepared for a long time as well. The pace of the construction was fast. Workmen were all over the building site as an anxiousness and excitement permeated the air.

The Temple furniture was put in place except for the Ark of the Covenant because it couldn't be found. It gave me insight into what I imagine may have something to do with the coming Millennium. The Ark of the Covenant won't be on their mind for the Prophet Jeremiah said, *"Then it shall come to pass, when you are multiplied and increased in the land in those days,"* says the LORD, *"THAT THEY WILL SAY NO MORE, 'THE ARK OF THE COVENANT OF THE LORD.' IT SHALL NOT COME TO MIND, NOR SHALL THEY REMEMBER IT, NOR SHALL THEY VISIT IT, NOR SHALL IT BE MADE ANYMORE."*

The sacrifices were restored beginning with the ashes of a red heifer according to the Old Testament. These sacrifices were not for salvation but were both sacramental and memorial in honor of Christ the Messiah who gave His life for the sins of the world. The sacrifices of the Old Testament pointed to the future salvation in the cross, and the sacrifices of the tribulation time pointed to the past salvation in the cross. They were sacraments that were most holy and sacred that honored the Son of God who was now a major part of the Jewish faith.

A Look Beyond

TWO WITNESSES

As the Temple was nearing completion, two men appeared that represented the Jewish nation. Most people thought that they were there to celebrate the building of the Temple, but they were there for quite another purpose. They were there to be witnesses for the living God and His plan for the Jewish people. We were told that Samuel was one of the first ones to see the witnesses and talk with them. No one knew where they came from. They just showed up. Just as the final working days on the Temple were coming to an end they began observing the structure and the workmanship. They looked pleased at what they saw. Samuel has been telling everyone "I believe that they are here to begin the operation of their ministry from the Temple area. When I first saw these men I immediately knew that there was something different about them. I believe that they are holy men of God."

Many others saw these men as well as Samuel, and still others saw them either on their television sets at home or on their pocket size phones that everyone carried with them. They were authoritative men that seemed to have the same kind of power that equipped the lives of the Old Testament Prophets. Everyone was astounded because these men were bold and didn't seem to be afraid of anyone or anything.

People were talking and saying that one of them resembles the ministry of Elijah the prophet. I remembered a teaching I heard in church years ago that Malachi the prophet said *"Behold, I will send you Elijah the prophet before the coming of the great and dreadful day of the LORD: And he shall turn the heart of the fathers to the children, and the heart of the children to their fathers, lest I come and smite the earth with a curse."*

Samuel thought that one of them was Elijah, and I had a tendency to agree with him. I know one thing, the only way hearts were going to turn to each other would be due to the horrendous tribulation that everyone was going through. They needed each other so they were clinging to family and friends as well. It was that bad! This time of indignation was and is a curse! Maybe hearts would turn to each other more so when this was all over. I don't know. At least I thought, God wasn't going to destroy us all!

The Jewish believers are spreading the word that yes indeed it was the ministry of Elijah that was to return to earth in the last days. Some believers are saying that the other prophet resembles the ministry of Moses while still others say that he resembles the ministry of Enoch. Either way, these men seem to hold the key to the power of God as they are performing mighty miracles. They are witnessing every day about the coming Kingdom of God. The people who were converted to God because of the ministry of the 144,000 were instant believers and followers of the two prophets. Others were skeptical and were not sure if they should put their trust in something that was so contrary to their past belief system.

I remembered that when I was a young man, one of my Bible teachers mentioned that God has two earthly men who always stood by the Lord's side. They were a witness of the miracles and control that God has over all the earth. It came back to my mind that the Bible said that there were those who were *"the two anointed ones that stand by the Lord of the whole earth."* I thought that was a powerful argument of verification that even God Himself had witnesses to display His mighty works and power. A friend of Samuel shared that scripture with him and he was overjoyed because it shed a light on what he was seeing in these men. The witnesses were pointing to Jesus Christ and he became a believer in what these witnesses were saying.

The two witnesses during this tribulation time spoke words that came out of their mouths like fire and it destroyed the vain arguments that their enemies had. If anyone tried to harm them the powerful words of these witnesses would cause them to die almost immediately. Their hearts would fail them from fear that destroyed them. What an amazing sight that was. At that point, I was happy to be on the Lord's side.

The witnesses had power to call on rain to come down from the heavens and they also had power to make it stop. When they did make the rain stop, serious drought ensued and everyone was angry with them including the leaders of many of the nations. When they wished, they turned the drinking waters of the earth to a ghastly putrid smell and a sickening blood-like contamination. It was awful. They spoke and diseases and viruses infected millions of people all around the world. They were in plenty of trouble yet they continued with their ministry. Their confidence was in God whom they trusted.

DEATH TO THE WITNESSES

This went on for about three and a half years and finally, people were getting annoyed with what they were doing. They were angry. They "had it with them" and wished that someone could do something with them like, put them in jail or kill them. People rioted and demanded the leaders to confront them. Eventually, the one man that everyone had trusted in, that I had suspected was the Antichrist, killed them both. He sent an army to surround them in Jerusalem where they were witnessing and his army destroyed them in the city streets._

Everyone was so upset with these two witnesses that no one seemed to care and no one buried them but just let their bodies lie in the streets. People would walk past them in disdain and mock their dead bodies and jeer at them as if they could hear them. Everyone from all around the world saw them on television or the internet and even on their phones they carried with them. They were so happy about their murder that to celebrate, everyone began to give each other gifts just like it was Christmas. They did this for three and a half days.

Then all of a sudden the two dead prophets began to stir and move. People began to panic as they all ran for cover. There was a dreadful worry that fell on everyone. Those who were watching on television began to cry and fear for their lives even though they may have been hundreds or thousands of miles away. No one knew what these men were going to do. Then, as quick as a blink of an eye they stood on their feet and a voice called them to heaven. They disappeared in a cloud and they were gone. They were taken up into heaven. Wow! It was amazing. Just like that, they were gone!

My spirit leaped in me as I felt that there was hope for my return to heaven. My prayer was, "God, don't leave me in this mess here on earth. I can't take it anymore. I want to return to be with you and my family. I want to be taken back to heaven just like these two witnesses ascended back to heaven. I want to bask in your presence and enjoy the praises with all of the other people of God. I know that this is impossible but please Lord, give me another chance and remember me in my time of affliction."

I wished that I could have shared my experience with Samuel of when I was in heaven and then told by God to return to earth, but we were miles apart, and he wouldn't understand anyway. So I kept my mouth shut and told no one else and kept the pain and grief to myself. Even though I was still on earth, my being in heaven even for the brief time that I was there, was precious to me. I was weeping as I wanted to return to heaven.

In the midst of my cries, a massive earthquake happened in the city of Jerusalem as thousands of people were killed. Ten percent of the city was reduced to nothing. Many homes and businesses were destroyed. I was concerned for the newly constructed Temple and for many people who lived in the city but I saw on television that the Temple had no damage. Many others were afraid as well but there were some in the city of Jerusalem that gave glory to God. These were ones who had believed in the ministry of the 144,000 and were now committed believers themselves. Others around the world were giving God praise! Technically and tragically, this was the end of what was called the second woe.

KINGDOMS OF OUR LORD

Then I saw clearly in my spirit and I personally rejoiced because I heard the announcement of the seventh angel. This was the third and final woe. To my great surprise I sensed a deep sense of relief as the angel announced along with many other voices of Heaven, *"The kingdoms of this world are become the kingdoms of our Lord, and of his Christ; and he shall reign for ever and ever."* Even though this was a wonderful announcement to my ears and to the believers during this time, it was horrible for the world. This seventh and final plague that was just pronounced on the earth was a trumpet of wrath and woe.

It was a vision in anticipation of the end of the Great Tribulation as if it had already occurred. I heard everyone in heaven including the twenty four Elders as they were rejoicing and praising God. In my spirit I saw the throne room of God in heaven. There the twenty-four Elders fell before the throne of God and they began to praise God. They lifted their hands and began to shout with all of the might, *"We give thee thanks, O Lord God Almighty, which art, and was, and art to come; because thou hast taken to thee thy great power, and hast reigned."*

I sensed their praise and it was beautiful, but there was going to be great punishment to the nations and its leaders on earth before that happened. The nations were angry because of the Divine indignation of God. I soon realized that the nations were showing their disdain and displeasure because God was about ready to judge them. The leaders of these nations were upset as the wrath of God was being fulfilled. They did not want God to interrupt their plans. The nations of the world hated everything that was happening.

Despite the sounding of this seventh trumpet of woe by the angel, I felt that it was a glorious time that never seemed to end, nor did I want it to end. This announcement was only an indication of the future reign of God in all the earth and also in heaven once the tribulation was over. God was just beginning to show that His desire is to make a perfect condition on earth like no human was ever able to do. He was going to control sin and make it possible for life to be at a time of peace, joy and eternal happiness.

In this vision of the future I saw the dead as they were judged and rewards given to prophets of old and the saints of God who were in awe of Him. The time had come for the righteous to rule during the 1,000 year reign of Christ on the earth. I saw the evil ones who had created violence and destruction in the earth judged for their sins. The believers in heaven all had an awesome understanding of God in their lives. Everyone from the smallest to the greatest, from the richest to the poorest felt relieved that God was going to punish those who had little value for the earth and those who did not understand the right way to manage it without sin.

TEMPLE OF GOD OPENED IN HEAVEN

I was astounded by what I saw next. *"The temple of God was opened in heaven, and there was seen in his temple the ark of his testament: and there were lightnings, and voices, and thunderings, and an earthquake, and great hail."* I knew right away that this announcement of the opening of the Temple of God in heaven was because of the announcement of the coming of the Lord's Kingdom, and for preparation of the next series of judgments that were soon to fall on the earth called the seven last plagues. This was the beginning of the end.

When I saw the Temple of God in heaven opening wide, it was the most marvelous sight that I could have ever imagined. For one thing, everything on earth seemed to move as all things were affected by an earthquake, voices, lightning, and hail. It was then that I understood that there really was no physical Temple in heaven because the Lord God Almighty and the Lamb are the Temple. All of those changes were coming from Him. He was opening up to the world.

God and the Lamb made up to be what was the core and strength of the Temple. What it seemed to me was that I was seeing the personality and characteristics of God that were being opened and displayed, and it was not anything physical. I saw His Divine presence that could only be described as more impressive than the most immense ornate cathedral. God was being revealed to me like never before.

It seemed that His attributes of love, mercy, grace and life were now a part of my own life. His never failing love was deep and abiding. His mercy extended to my deepest understanding. His grace was rich and plentiful to my soul. His life was resurrection and power. I was a part of Him and He was a part of me. I now understood the words of Jesus, *"abide in me, and I in you."* I felt that I could get to know God as He knew me. I saw Him as God who did not change which was far different than my life on earth that had continually changed.

I recalled the wonderful promise in God's word that says *"... they shall not teach every man his neighbor...know the Lord: for all shall know me, from the least to the greatest."* That's the feeling I have now. No one needed to show me how to know the Lord, I just knew Him. Without a word being spoken, everyone felt the same way as I did. Just being with Him was beyond the loftiest explanation that words could tell. I wanted to lay prostrate before Him in silence and awe because of His overwhelming power that was being poured into me. I was being inundated with Him as the source of all life.

The Ark of His Testament wasn't physical either, but it was His Holy presence that I saw just like the presence of God was upon the Ark of the Covenant in the Old Testament. God's Spirit and presence was touching the Holy Spirit that was abiding in me. His Spirit was totally surrounding the Spirit in me. Then it dawned on me, His presence permeated the entire heavens. There were no words to explain this other than the fact that God was revealing His holiness and righteousness to all of us. In His Testament I saw what His will and covenant of assurance was to His creation. God was getting ready to make His next move through His authority and wrath.

I was now beginning to understand why God sent me back to earth. I thought, things were hopelessly spinning out of control but I now knew that God was in control! When the power of the Devil and the Antichrist will be fully revealed, then the seven last plagues will fall on the earth. For some reason, God wanted me to know and witness this.

Soon I realized that there were more things that I had to take care of as my mind came back to reality on earth. What I saw was a revelation of His rightful heavenly claim to the earth through His might and power, and the wrath that was to come.

Chapter Twelve: Satan's Last Gasp

As my mind and thoughts had returned once again to earth, I knew that time was getting short as the horrible events of the Great Tribulation were taking place. How much more could the earth endure without being totally destroyed? How much more was God going to allow? I had no idea but I was interested in finding out.

My understanding seemed to be racing a thousand miles an hour as my mind tried to grasp those questions. I talked to some of the Jewish people that were protected by God in these awful days that we were living. I knew a few of them that were here in America. Some of them had become my close friends. They were telling me that they were having visions of the nation of Israel and that God was trying to bring them to an understanding of who the Messiah was and it was the Great Tribulation that was going to do just that. Many of them had the same vision night after night, over and over again. They shared it with each other and they could not get over the fact that the vision was the same with everyone.

Wow I thought, what was the vision? I asked my Jewish friend Nathaniel and he said that the vision that thousands of Jewish people were seeing was of God reaching out to the nation of Israel to prove that Jesus Christ of the New Testament was the

Messiah. They were saying both politically and spiritually, the nation of Israel was going to believe and follow Him as the Son of God. I thought, how wonderful that would be. Once again I recalled in Romans that it said, *"...all Israel shall be saved: as it is written, there shall come out of Zion the Deliverer, and shall turn away ungodliness from Jacob: for this is my covenant unto them, when I shall take away their sins."*

THE WOMAN IN THE SUN

When talking with Nathaniel, I asked him if he had any visions of Israel as well and if he did, what they were and what they meant. He told me that he and many of his friends said that in their visions they saw a woman in the heavens that they felt represented Israel. This woman had the sun wrapped around her like a garment of some kind. Nathaniel thought that the sun represented the brightness and strength of God's care for His people Israel. Many of his Jewish friends were excitedly talking about it. I was thrilled at their interpretation. I knew that God always took care of Israel.

I thought of an Old Testament scripture that I remember but really could never understand. It said *"But unto you that fear my name shall the Sun of righteousness arise with healing in his wings; and ye shall go forth, and grow up as calves of the stall."* Then it came to me. The strength and radiance of the sun wrapped around the woman they were seeing was like a sun-rise and ray of hope to the Jewish people. Their trial and healing would come as swift as being carried on a current of wings. Being right with God, they would return as a nation that would be strong as a young calf that would grow up protected by its mother. I was rejoicing with them.

He told me that in their visions this woman was standing on the moon and there were twelve stars like a crown on her head. Nathaniel explained to me that it was similar to the dream that

A Look Beyond

Joseph in the Old Testament had about him and his father and his brothers. It was a dream about a future time in his life when he was going to be a mighty leader over his family. It literally happened to him when he became the second in command to Pharaoh in the land of Egypt. That's why they connected their visions with the nation of Israel. It was all crystal clear to them.

I thought that what they were telling me made sense because I remember reading something about it in the book of Genesis. It was then that I knew that this all had to be more than just about Joseph and his rulership in Egypt and his reconciliation with his brothers. I asked myself, with the vision of this woman, did this mean that the nation of Israel and their plight was the center of all things that were happening in the world today? Of course, I knew that Jesus came from the tribe of Judah that was in Israel and that Mary gave birth to Jesus. That's what made me begin to understand.

With the moon under her feet, she would be as the power of the sun wrapped all around her and reflecting onto the moon that would eventually impact the world. The world would see her and all of her reflected beauty in their covenant relationship with God. The twelve stars representing the unity and control of the leadership of the nation of Israel would help her during this drastic time for her people. The world seeing the sun, moon and stars, would now see the importance of the nation of Israel. I was again astounded with this revelation and the fact that many of the Jewish believers were seeing the same vision.

Nathaniel further told me that many of them were having dreams concerning the time in the Bible when Jesus was born, and when Herod was jealous about Jesus and wanted to kill Him. He said that this was the work of the Devil who was really the one who wanted to see Jesus destroyed. The Devil had power over all of the nations of the past and he prompted Herod to try to destroy Jesus. The Devil and one third of the angels of heaven who were under his jurisdiction and had become evil, were seeking to destroy all of what God would do. Nathaniel and his friends now understood that Jesus was the Son of God and He ascended to Heaven and was soon to come back to the earth as the conquering Savior.

Nathaniel and all of the 144,000 who believed in Jesus were speaking about His coming future Kingdom. I recalled the scripture that said that Christ would rule with a rod of iron, meaning that He would be in control within all of the activity of His Kingdom and the kingdoms of the world. With this kind of excitement and vision by the Jews, I was thinking that during this awful period, the hope for the Jewish people would be running high.

However, Nathaniel and his friends were beginning to panic because of the pressure that was being put on the people of Israel causing them to leave their homes and flee to the neighboring country of Jordan. Some have moved and bought homes there. Others had moved elsewhere and have been living with friends and relatives. The Devil had inspired the Antichrist to speak anti-Semitic things against them by telling the nations of the world that Israel was responsible for many of the troubles that were happening today. The Antichrist was speaking many inflammatory and derogatory words that caused people to hate the influence that the Jewish people had in the world.

The Jews were compelled to leave just to escape the ravages and onslaught of the persecution. Their homes were being destroyed. They were being sent to jail. Their businesses were being closed for no reason at all. In some cases the Jews have been murdered. It reminded me of what Adolf Hitler did to the Jews in WW II when he killed millions of Jews. Not only did the Jews have to contend with what was happening to them, they still had to deal with the animosity, hatred and contention that there was between themselves and the Arab people who practiced their Islamic faith.

With the church gone, the Devil turned his anger on the Jews who were God's first love and covenant people. The Jews have been on the run just as in past years, and I now know from the book of Revelation that it was going to be for another three and a half years. It just doesn't look like there is any end in sight to the torture that was being leveled at them. The Devil-inspired Antichrist had tried to convince the other nations of the world to try and do something with the misplaced Jews who were there in Jordan, but the government of Jordan wasn't having anything to do with it.

Jordan was a neighboring nation of Israel and was of a more moderate Islamic faith, and has been kind to the Jewish people. They hid them and helped them as they escaped to their country. With the likelihood of war with Jordan, the Antichrist doesn't want to risk an invasion there in an attempt to destroy the Jews because of Jordan's treaty with the United Nations. He has been attempting to kill as many of the Jewish people as possible in other parts of the world.

WARFARE IN THE HEAVENS

Once again I was taken by the Spirit into the heavens and there I saw this tremendous warfare going on and the people in heaven around the Throne of God seemed noticeably concerned. Michael, who is the archangel that protects the children of Israel, was in a powerful battle with the Devil in the heavens above the earth and throughout the universe. He and his angels were battling the Devil and his angels.

A massive struggle was taking place from planet to planet and from galaxy to galaxy and throughout the numerous amounts of constellations. Stars were being knocked out of place. Planets were being thrown out of orbit and some were exploding. Fire was tracing across the heavens. Comets were coming dangerously close to the earth. Some were hitting the earth and exploding in bits and pieces in many of the nations. People on earth saw what was happening in the universe above them and many of them were scared. They didn't know anything about this powerful battle for control of the heavens between Michael and the Devil because they didn't see it.

The Devil and the one third of the angels that fell into sin with him thousands of years ago, and who were cast out of the throne room of God, were now cast to the earth. The Devil's work as the prince of the power of the air had come to an end. His full strength was now forced upon the earth for his final quest to try to destroy Israel and overthrow God. From that moment on, things were different. Nothing was the same. It's like you could sense something in the air.

I could feel that whatever was difficult to endure before, it was going to get worse in the future. You could sense the evil and the tension in the air. It was as if the Devil was having more sway and power on the earth. I remember reading in the book of Revelation that in the middle of the tribulation he was going to be cast down to the earth as a horrible time was predicted for the people of the earth.

In the dreams that the Jews had, the Devil had seven heads just as it says in the book of Revelation, which meant that he had been associated with seven of the most evil empires of history. He was now doing his best, or should I say his worst, to annihilate the Jewish people. These seven empires of the past all had something to do with the nation of Israel, whether good or bad. God had used each of them to deal with His covenant people. That's why the book of Revelation had pictured the Devil with seven heads. Now I knew that God had put a plan in place to bring His 'elect' back to Himself.

A Look Beyond

With my mind back here on earth I drove all the way home and rushed to find my Bible. I had to look and see what the book of Revelation said about all of this. Would I be able to find the passage that fit the time that the world was passing through now? How can I help my Jewish friends and anyone else that I may encounter to believe that Jesus Christ is returning to the earth soon? There was a struggle going on for the survival of the human race and I knew that there wasn't much time left. In the past, the Devil could not destroy God, and God would not destroy the Devil, but now the believers helped decide the victory through being overcomers!

Then I found a scripture in the book of Revelation that spoke volumes to me. As great alarm and joy gripped my mind and heart I read, *"I heard a loud voice saying in heaven, Now is come salvation, and strength, and the kingdom of our God, and the power of his Christ: for the accuser of our brethren is cast down, which accused them before our God day and night. And they overcame him by the blood of the Lamb, and by the word of their testimony; and they loved not their lives unto the death. Therefore rejoice,* ye *heavens, and ye that dwell in them. Woe to the inhabitants of the earth and of the sea! For the devil is come down unto you, having great wrath, because he knows that he hath but a short time."* What a powerful verse that scared me into praying all the more for the nation of Israel. This was their time to be overcomers!

JEWS ON THE RUN

A powerful persecution was directed toward the Jewish people that were in Jerusalem and in all of Israel. The Devil must have been very angry because it seemed that there was an all-out pursuit of the Jews as they were fleeing in all directions. This hatred had been going on for three and a half years of the tribulation. The Devil knew that time was running out and what he could direct in anger toward God and His people, he would have to do quickly.

Many Jews began to be scattered around the world and many more of them were still fleeing to the wilderness in Jordan where others were living. The Devil was determined to undermine God's everlasting covenant that He has with the nation of Israel and with Isaac, one of God's great children. As the scripture said, *"My covenant will I establish with Isaac."*

Israel was the one nation in the world that had a Biblical covenant with God that was established in the book of Genesis. They were the keystone nation that pointed to the soon return of Jesus Christ. Everything that God was showing me and that I was passing through in the Great Tribulation had everything to do with God's chosen and covenant people.

I was concerned for my Jewish friends that I had recently met. My thoughts and prayers were for Benjamin, Andrew and Nathaniel whom I knew were being used by God but would more than likely be facing severe persecution. I was guessing that they were on the run but I knew that they could not be killed because of God's special seal of protection upon them and the rest of the 144,000 who were the special servants of God.

Also, the Devil could do nothing about the Jews who had fled to Jordan. None of them could be captured or killed because of Jordan's treaty with the United Nations. I was hoping that the people of Israel whom my Jewish friends knew, had fled there too. I wasn't sure about many of the others who fled to other parts of the world. The Jews who fled, would have to remain where they were until things quieted down in the Jerusalem area.

The Devil influenced demonic filled people to circulate a flood of propaganda to try and turn the rest of the world in hatred toward these runaway Jews. The world was beginning to see what was happening so they did nothing evil to them. They weren't believing any of the propaganda and before long the threat was gone. I knew that God would protect His people because of the promise in the Bible that said, *"When the enemy shall come in like a flood, the Spirit of the Lord shall lift up a standard against him."*

The Devil was very upset because he could not kill those who had escaped so he turned his attention to those Jews who were still living in Israel. He especially persecuted those who had become believers in Jesus Christ because of the witnessing of the 144,000 members of the tribes of Israel. He went after new Christians and those who were completed Jews who were obedient to the commandments of God. I was reminded of the words of Jesus about the severe persecution of the Jews, *"They shall put you out of the synagogues: yea, the time cometh, that whosoever kills you will think that he doeth God service. And these things will they do unto you, because they have not known the Father, nor me."*

Chapter Thirteen: Against Christ

The one who has become known in the world during the past several years as a great leader is now looming larger than life as the Antichrist. He seems more Devil-inspired than ever before. Just like the Devil, he too is pictured in the book of Revelation as having seven heads. Through his association with the Devil, he seemed to glory in the fact that he was a product of the seven past empires that were connected with the nation of Israel in the past just like the Devil. He wanted nothing but harm to come to the Christians and the Jews who became believers in Christ. His reign as the most powerful man on earth is no different than some of the past leaders that persecuted the Jews. I know somehow that demonically he is connected to them in some way.

He was very similar to all other Antichrists of the past. His identity was with all of their kingdoms. Past Antichrist-like leaders took power over vast kingdoms that came to life under their authority. Everyone thought that those past kingdoms would never be heard from again but the Antichrist in the tribulation became the leader of a powerful kingdom that resembled the Egyptian, Assyrian, Babylonian, Persian, Greek, and the Roman Empires. It was from their territories that he had full recognition and power. It was as if one of his heads that was wounded came

113

back to power and life again. He then became the central leader over ten other powerful nations that were in league with him. His kingdom spread over all of the European and western world.

Suddenly, something devilish happened. People from practically everywhere began to believe that he was like a god. I met a woman by the name of Barbara who lived near me, and she said "I believe in him and what he can do for America and the rest of the world." She hung on every word that he spoke on television and over the internet. Some people were afraid of him but Barbara thought that he was the answer to all of the world's problems. His Teflon personality seemed to resist any criticism that came his way. Some people who worshipped him even began to ask, *"Who is like the beast? Who is able to make war with him?"* They thought that he was invincible. They just didn't see his beast-like nature. For years, he was the problem solver for the turmoil that the world was is.

He was the world's answer man. His idolization went on for a number of years. Then, all of a sudden that seemingly nice exterior personality that everyone at first fell in love with began to change. He broke the seven year protective plan that he helped to bring to fruition three and one half years ago. Overnight his demeanor changed to this devilish man that began to speak against the God that others in past years loved and adored. Now he was proclaiming that he was God. He became the one *"who opposes and exalts himself above all that is called God or that is worshiped, so that he sits as God in the temple of God, showing himself that he is God."*

He was blasphemous toward God and toward any other god that the world was worshipping. If my memory serves me right, after being known and respected over the past three and a half years, his power as the Antichrist was to last another three and a half years. He spoke openly against the God in heaven and against all those who proclaimed themselves as Jews or Christians. I was once again taken back by what the scripture says in Revelation that *"All that dwell upon the earth shall worship him, whose names are not written in the book of life of the Lamb slain from the foundation of the world."*

He began to persecute and make war with anyone who identified with the Jewish people or who called themselves Christian. He ruled the world with an iron fist. He overcame multitudes of people and many nations had to succumb to him. More and more people began to worship him and hang pictures of him in all of their government buildings. I began to realize that those who worshipped him were only those who did not become believers of Christ in the tribulation. Other than the Christians, the rest of the world followed him. This is where the faithful ones of the Lord were separated from the unfaithful ones. The faithful saints of God were patiently waiting for deliverance. They were expecting the soon return of Christ to the earth.

THE PERSONAL PROPHET

The Antichrist had a right hand man. He was his personal prophet. How easy it was for people to be seduced by him into thinking that the Antichrist was God. This false prophet was like a Doctor Jekyll and Mr. Hyde. I remember that the book of Revelation had described him as having two horns. I guess that was because he was gentle as a lamb but spoke like an evil dragon. His bipolar personality displayed his two diametrically opposed natures.

He came to the world supporting the Antichrist speaking comforting words of peace and assuring everyone that things about himself were on the up and up, but deep down he was a man who wanted to bring evil things to the world. He began to speak personal prophecies over the Antichrist when they were together. He prophesied "the Antichrist is God and there is no one like him that can help the needs of the people." It was like he was in a trance of some sort when he continually lifted up the Antichrist and encouraged people to worship him.

A number of months went by and I ran into Barbara again. She began to have second thoughts about this great man that she believed was the answer to every social ill that the world had. She heard his prophet speak prophetic words on television when he was at arena gatherings where he was the main speaker, or at any other place where people gathered together to understand more about the Antichrist. He certainly wasn't a believer in the creator God but he believed that the Antichrist was God. He too worshipped the Antichrist just like everyone else did. Something began to awake inside of Barbara. She questioned some of the things that the false prophet was saying. She came to me and said "there has to be a God that is above what this prophet was saying. He has to be a false prophet!"

She had seen that this prophet seemed to have natural yet supernatural abilities. He was both religious and political. She knew that he was forcing people to worship the Antichrist. She began to see right through the special relationship that the prophet had with the worldly leadership of the Antichrist. She was upset that he began to close churches and synagogues whenever and wherever he could. Those that he couldn't close, he attempted to confiscate possessions such as the homes and businesses of those who attended any form of worship center. He would work with banking institutions to make it difficult for anyone to purchase anything because they didn't worship the Antichrist.

She began to be sympathetic to those who were facing these financial difficulties. I could tell that her heart was becoming softer and changing from what she saw that was taking place in the world. Thankfully, the Holy Spirit gave me an understanding of her condition and I was able to lead her in a sinner's prayer. She began to believe in Christ as her Savior. I shared with her the scripture that said, *"That if you confess with your mouth the Lord Jesus and believe in your heart that God has raised Him from the dead, you will be saved" and "Therefore, if anyone is in Christ, he is a new creation; old things have passed away; behold, all things have become new."*

Her faith took her above the confusion that she was facing about the Antichrist and helped her believe in the God of the universe that captured her heart and mind. She was now fully living for Him. She began to profess Christ and say "my eyes have been opened." That put her in a dangerous position because of her new found faith but she continued speaking about Christ.

The false prophet that she was now wary of seemed to have magical powers. He was deceiving people by calling down fire from heaven as if he was some great godly man. Barbara and I didn't know how he was doing it but he was using fire to burn people and their possessions. She asked me, "How was that possible?" I told her, "He must be receiving help from the various evil demonic powers that still seemed to have some influence in the world after they were cast out of the heavens."

The false prophet also began to deceive people by performing miracles right in front of their eyes. He was performing miracles like rescuing people from the earthquakes, fires and other disasters that were taking place during this time. He had influence among the nations when they gathered together and when they met for their summit meetings. He was always speaking about the Antichrist and glorying in all that the Antichrist did.

THE IMAGE AND MARK

He called on people all over the world to make images to the Antichrist. He even forced the Jews in Jerusalem who had just completed their temple a few years before this to place an idol to the Antichrist in the center area of their worship. It was like he had it erected overnight. The idol was computerized to be able to speak and he insisted that everyone should worship this idol. I remember reading the words of Jesus where he gave a warning about seeing *"...the abomination of desolation, spoken of by Daniel the prophet, standing where it ought not..."*

The Jewish people were aghast! This caused some of the Jews to react violently against the Antichrist but they could do nothing about it. He killed those who didn't worship the idol but others had to flee Jerusalem and run to wilderness areas to get away from the Antichrist and his false prophet. Times were getting desperate for all of them.

All of that wasn't even the worst of it. The economy of the world was stagnant. Nations were in financial hardship all over the world. The economies of the world were all tied together. There was deep depression everywhere. In order to get a handle on the economy, the Antichrist's right hand prophet developed a system in order to keep track of all spending. They tried to get as many involved with this process as possible.

He attempted to keep control of all of the fraud that was hitting the markets of the world. He had to get control of the problems with credit cards so he developed a marking system. The government's seal or mark would be placed somewhere on the body of the person who would normally use a credit card. It was a mark that totally identified the person who was using it and no one else could use it. The only one who could use it was the bearer of the mark that was on the person's body.

The choice was given to the individual that they could decide to have a hidden mark or a tattoo displayed either on their right hand or on their forehead. The hidden mark was placed on the body by a laser beam so that it was not able to be seen with the naked eye. Those who chose the tattoo type of mark wore the mark with pride as it could be readily seen by everyone. The marks that were invisible, seen only by a scanner, or the tattoo type of mark that could be seen with the naked eye, were both a form of physical identity or sign for soldiers to see who was on the Antichrist's side. I heard one man on television say about the Antichrist, "I am proud to be identified with such a charismatic man of great stature and authority."

There was an announcement that was made that no one could *"buy or sell, save he that had the mark, or the name of the beast, or the number of his name."* This astonished everyone as it put a burden on many because they had to go to the government officials in each country or state in order to have the mark tattooed or branded on their body. Some counties were cooperating with the system while there were some who were not. A great monetary strain was put on the countries that were not in full cooperation with the Antichrist. Some countries were trying to create their own trade agreements centered on their cooperation with each other.

The only way that anyone could escape this financial difficulty was to move to a place that the Antichrist had perhaps little or no influence and to grow your own food and rely on yourself for other needs. For those who went on their own, it was very difficult to buy anything else that one would need to sustain themselves. The Antichrist had such a tight grip on the economy that those who wanted to sustain themselves had to be creative in order to survive. Various news organizations were tied in with the Antichrist and were part of those who were trying to expose the non-cooperative individuals and nations.

Also, there was a black market for food and other goods during the tribulation. Christians had to find out about these items in order to purchase them. People were travelling or moving to parts of the world where it was easier to access food. The security of many individuals had been breached by agents of the false prophet to find those who were opposed to the Antichrist.

A Look Beyond

The personal information on their phones was compromised and exposed.

There was a glaring difference of ideology between those who took the mark and served the Antichrist and those who did not take the mark and were serving the true Christ. Extra care was needed because those who had taken the mark were trying to expose those who had not taken the mark. A great persecution came upon those who were not aligned with the Antichrist's program.

The strange thing is that the Antichrist's mark was the number 666. Once I heard that, I sensed that the Antichrist had to be a man and not just a system because man was created by God on the sixth day and then fell into sin. For another thing, the number six is one number short of the number seven, used by God for completion in the Bible. Also, the number six is rendered three times which is the number used in the Bible for unity or perfection. I then realized that the Antichrist represented by the number six is the total embodiment of evil and destruction, which is just short of perfection in God represented by the number seven. I knew that he and his personal prophet were inspired by the evil of the Devil.

Chapter Fourteen: The Announcements

I n my spirit I was once again brought back to Heaven. I saw one of the most amazing and wonderful sights of all time. It took my breath away! The 144,000 who were the servants of God throughout the time of the Great Tribulation had now been translated to heaven some time at the end of the tribulation. The name of the Father in heaven was written on their foreheads to serve God for all eternity. The noise of this tremendous choir of 144,000 were accompanied by those playing on harps. Their singing was as the sound of powerful flowing waters and claps of thunder.

What a sight it was as they were singing the praises of God. The 144,000 were the only ones that could sing this song because they were the only ones who knew it. They were part of the ones who were set aside by God during the Great Tribulation and were the first to be taken from the earth to their place in heaven. Their speech was so perfect while on earth that they stood faultless in front of the throne of God and in the presence of the Lamb of God.

They sang this song in front of the four living creatures and the twenty-four elders. It held a special place in the heart of God. They were part of the ones who were redeemed from the earth. These special faithful servants of God were never married and they followed the leadership of the Lord throughout their time in the Great Tribulation. They did the work of the Lamb of God wherever He led them.

THREE ANGELS

Then, as quick as a flash, I found my spirit once again on earth. It was at this point that I realized that the situation on earth became so grave and so evil that the necessity to preach the gospel was critical. With the 144,000 gone, and instead of only men and women preaching, I looked up and saw an angel that God had equipped to bring heavy influence on the preaching of the everlasting gospel to every nation, language, tribe, and people. Nation after nation was encouraging freedom everywhere in allowing the gospel to be spread, despite the Antichrist.

There was a mixed condition in the world where it was easy to find the gospel message being spread but difficult to preach it because of the severe persecution. It was almost like you had to be in the right place at the right time in order to hear the gospel and be saved. But I knew God's Spirit was there to call people and there would be many that would respond to His call.

News reports came in that the gospel was being spread much greater than ever before on television, internet, radio, newspapers and magazines. The amount of churches being opened everyday continued to increase dramatically around the world. The apostate churches that had missed being translated to heaven were still resisting the gospel message. However, it was being accepted in many parts of every nation and by many believers who were receiving it.

Some of the believing churches in those nations that were indifferent and cold to the gospel before the tribulation were now having great revival. People were coming to a saving knowledge as to who Christ was. In some parts of the world the church doors were open day and night. The church staffs were busy around the clock just keeping up with the prayer and counseling that needed to be done for those who did not take the mark of the Antichrist. Those who had not taken the mark were fearful and running for their lives.

Those who had been influenced by the 144,000 were now preaching in malls, in colleges and universities, and in open meetings right on street corners. It was truly amazing. I was able to observe many churches and their Pastors leading their flock and teaching them how to minister to those who were in need. Even though the persecution was intense and many were being thrown in jail and physically abused, the preaching was still going on. All of this brought great anger to the Antichrist. He began to more seriously persecute the believers.

All of that freedom to minister was short-lived as a severe turnaround then took place. The Antichrist began to place great restraints on those who were sharing the gospel of Christ. He began to shut the gospel down on the air waves and in the printed page. Many leaders and their people had to escape and preach where there was less restraint. The church where there were the true believers in Christ had to go into hiding. Much of the church was on the run. Many of the people who were serving Christ had to move the church to hidden places. The church was now going underground to meeting places in secret areas that were hidden in order to escape. It was a confusing and alarming time.

Then I understood why God had to use an angel to preach the gospel. The angel that God had sent was preaching the gospel message because much of the church was in peril. He was appearing all over the earth. It was like he was everywhere at the same time as if He was ever-present in a last ditch effort to tell everyone to give honor to God before it was too late. He would appear to multiple persons at the same time; in businesses, in family outings, from home to home, and even appearing to people at night in their bedrooms.

He was giving everyone one last chance and hope to believe in God so that they would be spared from eternal destruction and damnation. People from all over the earth seemed to be hearing this angel because he was speaking with a loud voice that was reverberating all over the earth. They had to make a choice to either serve God or face His judgment. The Antichrist could do nothing about it.

Some people were scared while others were astounded as they stood in awe at the sight of this magnificent angel. The result of his message was powerful as everyone seemed to be affected in some way, either to believe or reject his message. The angel was saying *"Fear God, and give glory to him; for the hour of his judgment is come: and worship him that made heaven, and earth, and the sea, and the fountains of waters."*

BABYLON IS FALLEN

I looked up and saw another angel flying with speed all over heaven, from nation to nation with a piercing message for all the world to hear. The news that he gave was powerful and prophetic as the entire political, economic, religious, and social systems were ready to collapse. The angel declared, *"...Babylon is fallen, is fallen..."* The announcement by this angel was piercing and it rang with authority and finality.

The entire system that was associated with the Old Testament system of Babylon was now coming to its end. There was panic and destruction everywhere. People were scared. The leaders of the nations were in a state of panic. Many financial institutions all over the world were collapsing. I'm not sure if anyone else saw this angel, but it was sad to hear the tidings of this tragedy.

David E. Siriano

Again I looked up and saw a third angel crying throughout the heavens declaring, *"...If any man worship the beast and his image, and receive his mark in his forehead, or in his hand, the same shall drink of the wine of the wrath of God...and he shall be tormented with fire and brimstone in the presence of the holy angels, and in the presence of the Lamb: and the smoke of their torment ascendeth up for ever and ever: and they have no rest day nor night, who worship the beast and his image, and whosoever receiveth the mark of his name."*

It was depressing for all those who fell into the trap that was set by the Antichrist. Those who had already received the mark were running scared as word was spread by believers about their punishment. There were so many people that received the mark that it was too difficult to estimate how many.

Despite the grave feeling that I had for the lost, I sensed a great amount of satisfaction for those that had given their lives in martyrdom. They stood their ground in the Great Tribulation, did not worship the Antichrist, and refused his mark. They endured their struggles, kept the commandments of God, stayed true to the Lord and were killed for their faith. They had to wait in patience during this time for God to take vengeance on their enemies, but they were rewarded with eternal rest knowing that their works will be remembered.

Sadly, I met a man named George who with his entire family had taken the mark of the Antichrist. When they were told of the consequences of their actions, they were deeply grieved. Someone showed them what it said in the Bible and they were physically shaken. They began to believe the information in the Bible and what Christians told them. They spoke to many people and visited churches to see if the mark could be removed. They were told that it could not. It was too late.

"We thought we were doing the correct thing for our entire family," they said. "We thought that we needed to take the mark to cooperate with the governmental system just to be able to buy groceries and make purchases." George and his wife were crying uncontrollably. They realized it and screamed "We are going to be eternally separated from God and tormented forever because we took this mark" as they pointed to their hands and foreheads. Their adult children were crying as well. It was heartbreaking.

We saw on television that people who took the mark in other parts of the world were visibly shaken as the message of this third angel somehow reached the world. They had been warned by Christians in their countries not to take this mark. Now they were sobbing with fear and depression. Leaders of those nations didn't understand the results of their actions and the actions of their people. Many of those leaders were atheists or agnostics at best. The people in those countries were now realizing their mistake and put the blame solely on the great leader of all the nations, the Antichrist.

HARVEST OF THE EARTH

Then I saw the most wonderful vision I had ever seen in my life. It was a vision of Jesus sitting on a cloud and He had a crown on His head and a sharp harvesting sickle in His hand. He was told by an angel with a loud voice that the time had come to reap the good harvest of the earth. He thrust the sickle into the earth and harvested all of the good grain of the earth. The good grain represented all of the Godly people at the end of the Great Tribulation. The time had come for the earth to be harvested and the earth was reaped of all the good people of the earth to meet the Lord. This was it. This was the end.

Another vision appeared to me and I saw an angel who also had a sharp harvesting sickle in his hand. He was told by another angel who had control over fire, to also harvest the earth. This harvest was of the evil grain or evil people of the earth at the end of the Great Tribulation. The first angel gathered all of the evil clusters of the people of the earth and cast them into the winepress of the wrath of God.

This picture of evil people being cast into the winepress of the wrath of God became a picture of when God would gather all the nations of the world together for a battle called Armageddon. This vision of Armageddon appeared to be so devastating that I somehow felt that I would see it over and over again. I thought to myself that this was going to be another world war. The Lord wanted me to see the massive bloody destruction that was to come.

MY FIRST VIEW OF ARMAGEDDON

The Armies that were gathered at the end of the Great Tribulation were poised in all sections of the world. Armies were in the east from Asia, and in the north from Russia, and Europe. Armies were in Africa and the Middle East including the Arab terrorist groups. The battle was being waged for 180 miles and it extended from Megiddo in the north of Israel all the way south to Jerusalem and into Jordan were the Jews were hiding.

The nations were beginning to have troubles with each other and the Antichrist was right in the middle of all of it. He had much difficulty with many of them who were not under his direct control and authority. I recall what Daniel the prophet wrote about his troubles he would have at this time. Daniel says, *"But tidings out of the east and out of the north shall trouble him: therefore he shall go forth with great fury to destroy, and utterly to make away many. And he shall plant the tabernacles of his palace between the seas in the glorious holy mountain; yet he shall come to his end, and none shall help him."* This meant that his headquarters and his home were right in Israel and that's where he was being challenged. He certainly was having his difficulties as many nations that were not aligned with him posed severe problems for him.

On television I saw the bodies that were strewn for hundreds of miles with blood splattered as high as the heads of horses and the tops of tanks. This vision that came to me was so stunning and so evil that it took my breathe away. The battle went on for days, and then it carried on into weeks. At night, the battle subsided but then began again in the morning. At home, I laid awake for hours at a time. I got little sleep as I contemplated what God was going to do. I was scared for America, hoping that the battle would remain in the Middle East as the Bible had predicted.

I thought the Lord was supposed to return to earth during the battle of Armageddon. When He returned, the church would be with Him. I should be with Him when He returns but I have been stuck here on the earth during this awful tribulation. Where is He? He hasn't come yet. All of the armies of the world are gathered together. Where's my family? I didn't understand. I was confused. Maybe He will return toward the end of the battle. I just didn't know. I could only pray and beg God for His mercy.

The consolation I had was that I knew that the scriptures said *"The field is the world; the good seed are the children of the kingdom; but the tares are the children of the wicked one; the enemy that sowed them is the devil; the harvest is the end of the world; and the reapers are the angels. As therefore the tares are gathered and burned in the fire; so shall it be in the end of this world. The Son of man shall send forth his angels, and they shall gather out of his kingdom all things that offend, and them which do iniquity; and shall cast them into a furnace of fire: there shall be wailing and gnashing of teeth. Then shall the righteous shine forth as the sun in the kingdom of their Father. Who hath ears to hear, let him hear."* I also knew that the scriptures say *"Be patient therefore, brethren, unto the coming of the Lord. Behold,*

David E. Siriano

the husbandman waiteth for the precious fruit of the earth, and hath long patience for it, until he receive the early and latter rain."

Even though that promise is given in the gospels and it appears that the unrighteous is gathered first, just the opposite is true. The resurrection order according to the book of Revelation that was given to John was that the righteous are gathered first and then the unrighteous were gathered after that. I saw the same vision that God gave me and it was identical to what John saw. It was that first the righteous people were to be harvested and taken to heaven, and then the evil ones were to face the harvest of Armageddon and taken to hell. This was a serious time for the world as the wrath of God was now going to be completed. The world was reeling in its times of war and turmoil and no one knew what to do about it.

Chapter Fifteen: The Overcomers

SONG OF MOSES AND THE LAMB

A further vision unfolded before me of what was happening in the heavens and around the throne of God as I sensed a terror and horror like never before. It was then that I saw seven mighty angels that had seven hand-held containers of the last plagues of the wrath of God to the fullest in their hands. They were ready to pour out God's wrath upon all the earth. Before any of the wrath would be released by the angels, those who were the overcomers in the tribulation had to be accounted for, just like the 144,000 had been taken to heaven.

That's when I saw standing in front of the throne of God and on the transparent sea of glass of purity and holiness that was now mixed with fire, those who had gotten the victory over the Antichrist, his image, his mark, and the number of his name. They had refused his mark, his name, and did not bow to his image. They went through the fires of persecution, paid the price for it with their lives and were now standing on the sea of glass in front of God the Father.

In this vision of the end of the tribulation, I saw them with harps in their hands and they were singing the praises of God. The song was an anthem of Moses and of praise toward Jesus

David E. Siriano

Christ the Lamb of God. I then knew that this wasn't the true and believing church because the church doesn't sing the song of Moses and has never sung the song of Moses. These were Jewish people who were redeemed as well as those Gentiles who were influenced and saved because of the ministry of the 144,000 who were the servants of God.

All of them went through the Great Tribulation and were acknowledging Moses and his teaching and great leadership in the birth of the nation of Israel. They were also giving praise to Jesus Christ for His Messiahship and resurrection that was extremely important in the plan of redemption. They were also pointing to the 1,000 year reign of Christ on earth called the Millennium.

Both the saved Jewish people and the Gentiles who were saved during the Great Tribulation sang about the marvelous works of the Lord God that saved them from a life of despair and destruction. Their song was, *"Great and marvelous are thy works, Lord God Almighty; just and true are thy ways, thou King of saints. Who shall not fear thee, O Lord, and glorify thy name? For thou only art holy: for all nations shall come and worship before thee; for thy judgments are made manifest."*

Even though terrible calamity was falling upon the earth they still proclaimed that God was justified in allowing these evil deeds to transpire all over the world. They praised God for His holiness and knew that all people would fear Him and they proclaimed that all of the nations were going to worship Him because of His covenant with the nation of Israel.

TEMPLE OF GOD OPENED IN HEAVEN

Once again as part of my vision, the Temple of the Tabernacle of the Testimony of God open up in heaven. The Lord was ready to return to the earth. What I saw next was the representation

131

of the living God pouring out of the center of His Glory that surrounded the throne. I felt that the glory I saw was the very centerpiece of the presence of God as it was seen in the example of the Tabernacle that was given to Moses after He led the Children of Israel out of Egypt. I saw His brightness, dignity, honor and splendor that engulfed all of heaven. It had already been revealed to me that there really was no physical Temple in heaven because the Lord God Almighty and the Lamb are the Temple.

In this vision I saw myself not only in the throne room of the Father in heaven, I was in what I felt was the actual Tabernacle of God's nature in heaven, which was God Himself. It was the Temple of God and the Lamb. Coming from the very center of this throne and Tabernacle-like sense of His being in heaven, was a cloud of God's Spirit and a Holy Fire just like I read about in that Old Testament Tabernacle.

That presence permeated not only heaven but every living being that was now in heaven. It penetrated the very Spirit and Soul of every one there. I was taken aback with an indescribable sense that God was a part of everything. He was in everyone that knew Him, and He was there with a presence that made you feel like you were a part of God and He was a part of you. I was stunned with an all-consuming awe that would not leave me, nor would I want it to leave me.

I couldn't get over the fact that the Presence of God seemed to envelope me and everyone else that was in heaven. I sensed His omnipresence and omnipotence. I felt crowned with His goodness, immersed in His holiness, and sanctified by His righteousness as His love took hold of my soul and spirit. It grabbed me and wouldn't let me go! Just as Adam knew God's Glory and presence so powerfully that he was unaware that he was naked before he had sinned, I was unaware of any of my past shortcomings in my life on earth.

David E. Siriano

As I basked in this Holy Presence, a revelation of understanding came to me that the pattern of the Tabernacle in the Old Testament was constructed after the pattern that I was now sensing in heaven. I came to understand that it was only a shadow of the heavenly Tabernacle.

That was why Moses received such strict instructions about the design of the Tabernacle that would show the very presence of God in the Holy of Holies. Now that I saw this Temple of the Tabernacle in heaven, I remembered Hebrews chapter nine were it said that Christ was a *"greater and more perfect tabernacle not made with human hands"* and that *"He went once for all into the Holy of Holies of Heaven."*

It was impressed on my mind that the scripture said that the things of the earthly Tabernacle had to be purified by the blood of animal sacrifices but *"the actual heavenly things themselves required far better and nobler sacrifices"* referring to Christ that His sacrifice was far better. It says *"For Christ (the Messiah) has not entered into a sanctuary made with [human] hands, only a copy and pattern and type of the true one, but [He has entered] into heaven itself, now to appear in the [very] presence of God on our behalf."*

As I thought and meditated on all this, I came to the realization that the seven angels were now ready to pour out the seven last plagues of God's wrath on the earth as a continuation from the Temple of God being open before. They came right out of the Temple of God's presence in heaven after the previous seven angels sounded their trumpet judgments. These angels were dressed in white and the front of them was platted in gold. They were brilliant and shining with the reflection of the Glory of God that was only found in the Temple of God Himself.

They had golden containers that were filled with the wrath of God and were given to them by the four living Creatures that were in and around the Throne of God. They were going to pour their containers out on the earth. I knew that the end was near and that nothing but terror awaited those who were disobedient to God on earth. I wept in my spirit as I cried out in what I felt was total desperation. How was it possible that I could feel this way in heaven? But I knew that my feelings were real. From deep within my soul I felt, "Oh God, I don't think I can handle the despair that is soon to come."

The Temple in heaven was full of a smoke-like haze that swirled around the throne of God and from the Glory of His presence. The power of God was so great that no one could come into the Temple of His presence until the angels completed their mission. Everyone stayed clear of God during this moment. No one went near His throne. His wrath was so powerful and awesome that everyone in heaven could not even stand to be near the presence of God until this was over.

This was going to be disastrous for the earth but glorious in our relationship with God. I simply could not imagine what was going to take place on the earth as I felt this terrible horror that was coming from God. Seeing the Temple being opened before was the beginning of the end, seeing it opened for the second time was now the end. I was amazed as I realized what this moment meant for the world.

Chapter Sixteen: Judgment

SEVEN LAST PLAGUES

With my mind back on earth, I knew this was it. I sensed that coming from the Temple of God in heaven was an awful pronouncement that was about to take place. I saw seven angels that swooped in upon the earth and I could see by the look in their eyes that something horrific was about to take place. Each of these angels had what appeared to be gigantic containers that seemed to be filled with a colorful fiery red and orange substance that would have been too hot for any human to handle.

I wondered what they were going to do with those containers but it didn't take me long to find out. I thought no, it couldn't be. They were told to fly across the heavens and pour out the contents that were in their containers all over the earth. Yes, they were told to go, and one at a time and in an overlapping manner, to pour out their containers of wrath all over the land and sea. I knew that when they did that, it was going to be something that would drastically alter the landscape, the people and the nations of the earth. Each of these seven last plagues of judgment lasted for months. I could only imagine the screams that I was going to hear from everyone who lived in the area where these containers were going to be emptied.

A Look Beyond

The first angel went swooping down upon the earth and poured out his container on those who had taken the mark of the Antichrist and those who were worshipping him. Once again, offensive and disgusting sores inflicting grief and sorrow manifested themselves on their bodies. They were horrible sores that were offensively putrid to the smell. The skin of those with those sores were blistering and then falling off their bodies. Men and women were screaming with pain and revulsion. Many of those who had these sores were quarantined away from the masses of people who did not have the mark nor worshipped the Antichrist. The sores on the bodies of these unbelievers lasted for weeks and months. They could not get rid of these sores. Screams were heard everywhere you went. Many died in their grief and sorrow.

A family that I saw being interviewed on television were among those who were affected by the terribleness of this Divine wrath. They attended an apostate church on occasion so I don't think that they heard anything about the End-Times and what this terrible Antichrist would do. Their names were Tony and Michelle. They and their two teenage children had taken the mark offered by the Antichrist. They broke out with skin lesions that were very painful. They said, "We went to doctors and checked into emergency rooms but the wait was long as many others were ahead of us with the same sores. The pain is unbearable." The best that Tony and Michelle could do was to put a recommended cream on their bodies to try and relieve some of the painful sores. Their children could not attend school but even if they could, their school was closed because of the skin sores that everyone seemed to have. The infections had spread to many of the teachers as well. They were all to be separated from God and lost forever.

I was not affected by this terrible wrath because I didn't take the mark of the Antichrist. I had none of the sores nor the pain that so many other people had. I was immune to this condition because I was divinely protected. Once again I was afraid so I still prayed every day that God would protect me from this awful condition.

A second angel rushed over the oceans pouring his container out over the millions of miles of water all across the world. Then the waters turned blood-like because of the wars and the nuclear weapons that were used during the tribulation. The waters were thick with animal corpses that were floating in the waters and washing up on the shores. Similar to the second trumpet judgment when one third of the sea creatures died, now all the sea creatures died. The odor coming across the waters and over the waves with the power of wind currents was disgusting to the smell. Industrial shipping came to a standstill. Wars involving nuclear weapons continued to rage across the nations causing chemical reactions in the waters in every hemisphere. Nuclear warfare was a major part in this destruction just before the return of the Lord.

It was so sickening and repulsive that people who lived near the shores or were vacationing left in large numbers to get away from the water. Friends of mine, Rick and Elaine that I had met months earlier, were on vacation in Hawaii but left early because they could not enjoy the rest of their vacation. This prime vacation spot was affected by the blood soaked waters just like other parts of the world. "It was difficult for us to even find a flight home because everyone else was trying to escape the same dilemma as us" they said. "We have to get home to family and friends to get together with them and try to figure out a plan of survival."

The third angel emptied his container over the rivers and springs that held the drinking waters of the earth and they became contaminated all over the world. Similar to the third trumpet judgment when one third of the waters became bitter, now they all became blood-like in substance. Nuclear weapons not only destroyed the vast ocean waters of the world but much of the land areas as well. The drinking waters of the world had been devastated by the mass destruction. Water purifying plants that were still operating in some parts of the world had to work harder at cleaning the waters. It was something that the centers for disease control never experienced before and they had to find new methods to purify the waters. Scientists from some countries were sharing their findings with scientists in others countries so that people wouldn't die of dehydration. It was one of the most terrifying events on earth because of the seriousness of the situation, knowing that people cannot live but a few days without water. I was searching for water as well.

Many others were searching for bottled water too. Rick and Elaine escaped to the mountains and searched for streams that were far away from the affected rivers and fountains of waters. They were somewhat successful but day by day it was increasingly difficult to find even bottled water necessary for drinking as the contaminated waters increased in every direction.

The angel that was responsible for keeping the waters clean knew that this was a judgment that came from God. He knew that the wrath of God was being fulfilled. This was one of the worst events that could be placed on individuals and yet the angel knew that this was necessary. His words actually applauded God for taking vengeance out on the depravity and sin of the people of the earth.

The angel cried out *"You are righteous, O Lord, The One who is and who was and who is to be, because you have judged these things. For they have shed the blood of saints and prophets, and you have given them blood to drink. For it is their just due."* Then, a powerful voice of another angel came out of the altar of God that was in heaven that agreed with the judgment. He confirmed the action of God and cried out, *"Even so, Lord God*

Almighty, true and righteous are your judgments. " I heard their soul penetrating words of Divine punishment.

Then the fourth angel took his container and emptied it on the sun so that the sun's rays were intensified. The result was devastating. The heat was excruciating. It was so hot that it seemed like the sun had moved closer to the earth, although I knew that didn't happen. We were all scorched with a horrible heat as the temperature was raised all over the planet. Many received third degree burns from the raging heat that came from the sun. Oh, the humanity that cried out in pain and suffering! It was like watching the worst horror movie! This was global warming at its worse.

People couldn't escape the fires that were burning in all corners of the globe. They were severely burned yet they continued to cry out in anger toward God and swore in the name of God and showed no respect or repentance for their evil deeds. They felt no regret nor did they attempt to change their lifestyle or their way of life. They certainly did not ascribe to God any glory or praise. It was a pitiful time and awful to see!

With glee, the fifth angel threw the contents of his container on the kingdom where the Antichrist was in power. A heavy severe darkness permeated his kingdom which was just the opposite of the raging heat that was still affecting the rest of the world. The Antichrist ruled much of the world but there were many nations that were not under his control so they were not affected. The other kingdoms of the world did not have the severe darkness as the kingdom of the Antichrist. On television it was so dark that it was very difficult to even see anything that was transpiring in the Antichrist's domain.

The people of the Antichrist's kingdom were biting their lips and tongues because of the excruciating pain and torment. They were exhausted, lying in the streets and dying in droves because of the radical change, first from the heat and now the darkness. The darkness was so severe, they couldn't even see the hand in front of their face. They swore and cried out loud with horrible sores that they still had from the first plague and that they couldn't tend to, because it was so dark. Still, there was no repentance but only defiance toward God.

The angel who brought the darkness knew of the atrocities and viciousness of the Antichrist. He was delighted to be the angel in charge of this destruction. He knew how evil the spirit of the Antichrist was. As an angel who was on God's side, nothing made him happier than to see this kind of destruction happening to the kingdom of the Antichrist.

Now it was coming to the end of the Great Tribulation. I could feel the tension. The world was reeling from exhaustion. I once again recalled the scripture in Romans where it says, *"... the creation itself also will be delivered from the bondage of corruption into the glorious liberty of the children of God."* I thought, 'this was it.' I felt that even I wanted to hide myself from the anger of God. How could all of creation have gone this far from the original plan of God that He wanted in the Garden of Eden? How could it have gone this far from God that He would have to invoke such wrath? The end was coming and I felt it stronger than ever. I uttered in prayer, "Why was I here watching all of this? Oh God help me understand."

BATTLE OF ARMAGEDDON

Then it happened! The appearance of the sixth angel came and somehow I knew that this was going to be disastrous. This angel showed me a second view of the battle of Armageddon with the Devil, Antichrist, and false prophet just before the Second Coming of Christ. He emptied his container on the mighty river Euphrates, the river that was in the Garden of Eden with Adam and Eve. It was there to help sustain life in the early days of the creation of the world and now it would play a role in its destruction. The river bed was dry, the water was gone.

In the constant ebb and flow of the battles of Syria and Iraq, the dam that controlled the waters into Syria and Iraq were diverted in another direction. The great waters of the river Euphrates that flowed into the Persian Gulf was there no more. The scripture in Revelation was being fulfilled which said, *"That the way of the kings from the east might be prepared."*

On television I saw the armies of millions of soldiers that had been fighting in the Eastern nations ride and march through Iraq on the way toward Israel. The armies were fierce looking. They appeared strong and powerful. I recall seeing these armies earlier at the sixth angel trumpet announcement as they marched into the Middle East, starting wars involving many nations. Now they were marching into Israel and into Jerusalem. There were soldiers that walked, rode in jeeps, in tanks, all-terrain vehicles, mine resistant vehicles, and helicopters.

Other armies were coming from further north through Georgia and Syria, including armies that were from Eastern Europe and Russia. On news reports of television and the internet, the sight was almost unbelievable! What were all these armies going to do? How did they get so many men and women to gather together like that? Who were they going to fight and why were they marching into Israel? Was Armageddon actually going to come to pass?

Television and the internet were also reporting that some of the armies of the Russian Federation and Eastern Europe were being launched from the Crimean peninsula by ships and airplanes, and jets more specifically. Apparently, their plans are to have the ships flow through the Black Sea and into the Mediterranean Sea and launch missiles into Israel. I would assume that they will also send amphibious forces to land there as well.

Israel was standing alone as Arab nations also joined the fray. Terrorism at the heart of Islam, was rearing its ugly head in ways never thought possible before. The United States of America, my very own country, was no longer willing or able to help Israel as in the past. I'm afraid that we had been derelict in our duty to help preserve and protect God's covenant people from the Old Testament. I remember hearing in one of my Bible Classes that in the book of Obadiah, God was very upset with the Edomites because they stood by and did not help their brothers the Israelites when they were being plundered and taken from their land. I was afraid that the same thing was going to happen to America. I knew that even if a nation took a neutral stand in regard to Israel, it would pay the consequence of incurring the wrath of God. I was scared for America and prayed for her daily and fervently.

The situation around the world was getting so grave and dangerous. It seemed like the three anti-god individuals, the Devil, the Antichrist, and the false prophet were sending forth demonic like spirit signals into the world as a final showdown with God. These spirits performed signs and miracles to convince people from around the world of their power. Then they multiplied and began to inhabit and control leaders and their armies in every nation. *"For they are the spirits of devils, working miracles, which go forth unto the kings of the earth and of the whole world, to gather them to the battle of that great day of God Almighty."*

Things were getting scary! The nations around the world were on edge and in a state of panic. The armies in many of those nations were restless as they began to gather together. It appeared like they were against each other in a demonic state of confusion that came from those evil spirits. They only have themselves to blame because they had an unrepentant spirit. The focus of attention of these armies was the nation of Israel.

Then came a powerful voice that seemed to echo across the heavens, *"Behold, I come as a thief!"* The Lord was coming and He was ready to rescue the earth after this destruction. The armies of the world that were coming from the east and from the north were now gathering in Israel representing many religious entities. The fighting began and it was certainly intense. What I saw was inhumane as these warring nations came together and as John wrote, God *"...gathered them together into a place called in the Hebrew tongue Armageddon."*

As I saw on television, the armies that were coming from the east were from China, Korea, Japan, and Afghanistan. The armies of the north were coming from Turkey, Armenia, Georgia, and Azerbaijan and from across the Caucasus Mountains from the southern parts of the Russian Federation. Armies were also gathering from Europe and from the countries that were in northern Africa. The Arab countries also came against Israel with such vengeance because they had such a hatred for the Jews. The armies were so vast for me to know exactly how many.

All of these armies from the East and the North were a fulfilment of what the books of Revelation and Ezekiel prophesied. On television the site of them were unbelievable. It appears that they were gathering to fight against each other and against Israel. In the middle of the disaster that was coming to Jerusalem were people of the three major religions of the world that were now living in the Great Tribulation, namely Islam, Christianity, and the Jews. They had missed the earlier translation of the church to heaven.

A Look Beyond

IT IS DONE

The seventh angel poured out his container into the air and then came another voice from out of the sanctuary of heaven from the very throne room of God saying, *"...it is done..."* In other words, it was announced that it was all over, it is accomplished. I was passing through this just like everyone else. This was yet another picture that God gave me of the coming end. This was part of the coming of the Lord and I was thinking of my family and would be looking for them.

Throughout the heavens I heard voices, thunder and saw lightning. There also was an earthquake like there never was on the face of the earth since man was first created. The earthquake was like a chain reaction that followed the fault lines throughout Asia, North and South America, Europe, and Africa and all around the world. The earth seemed to be splitting apart. The earthquakes triggered landslides and volcanoes. Then there was one massive tsunami after another that affected every continent. There was nowhere on the face of the earth where people felt safe anymore as millions of people perished.

Nations on every continent were affected by this massive earth shattering event. It reached around the world as nations were politically and economically falling apart. God was furious at the nations of the world as He vented His wrath upon them. Nations fell under the weight of the mighty wrath of God as the Babylonian system was being dealt with by God's wrath. This was another picture that Babylon had fallen!

The earthquake was so powerful that the islands in the middle of the oceans sank beneath the waters causing many more deaths. The rocks of mountains fell into the valleys as the mountains were laid low with tremendous rumblings. The great earthquake was followed by huge hailstones that were about fifty to sixty pounds in size. The hailstones destroyed buildings, damaged property and killed many people in every part of the world as they were running for cover. Cities were destroyed in every nation and on every continent. It was difficult to hide as destruction was everywhere. The plagues of God were exceedingly great, yet the hearts of many of them were not right with God as they continued to swear at Him because of the torture that they were going through.

Chapter Seventeen: Fall of Political Babylon

I saw one of the judgment angels who had one of the seven containers. He began to speak about a woman whose seat of power was in the nations of the world and within the peoples of all those nations. She was so associated with all of their leaders that she is pictured as committing spiritual adultery with them and the nations that they represented. She wasn't political herself but she was riding on the back of the Antichrist and worldly politics, gaining all types of blasphemous titles and names. She was intoxicated with the abominations of their idolatry that put ungodly pleasures and ideas ahead of the one true God. This woman seemed far away from God and His commandments of holiness and righteousness.

I thought, "Oh no, not another vision of what would happen at the end! Now who could this possibly be? What could this possibly mean?" Her allegiance was to the nations and it seemed she had the authority and approval of the leader of all of those nations. When I looked carefully, that leader appeared to me to be none other than the Antichrist. The combined powers of the woman and the Antichrist ruled the nations of the world and held power over the fate of its people. The unfortunate thing was that it felt like to me that she was only being used by the Antichrist. Who knew whether or not the Antichrist would help her to achieve power or turn against her? I was astonished!

I was taken by the Spirit into the wilderness in the country of Jordan, and I saw the woman that the angel showed me. Just as I had seen, she was closely associated with the Antichrist that had been gaining power throughout the earth. She was riding with his authority and power. The Antichrist himself was associated with the Devil through the power of the seven biblical superpower nations of the past. The Antichrist was the head of a consortium of ten groupings of nations that he was heading up in the Great Tribulation that I was now living in.

The only thing that I could think about this woman is that she looked like she represented the apostate church in the tribulation. She was far away from the God that she was supposed to love and revere. The reason that I felt that this woman was the church was because she was clothed with beautiful robes of purple and red that was woven with gold, and she was decked out with all kinds of precious stones and pearls. Her clothing reminded me of the priestly robes that were worn by the spiritual leaders in the Old Testament. Before the believing church was translated to heaven, many other churches and world religions had come together for unity and cooperation who at best were lukewarm and at worst apostate. Instead of a relationship with Christ, they were now identified with the Antichrist and had an alliance with him.

She was holding in her hand a gold cup full of sinful practices that was a picture to me of all of the adulterous associations she had with all of the leaders of the world including the Antichrist. Instead of being in a pure relationship with the Christ she was supposed to serve, she was filled with abominations of idolatrous offences and unrepentant crimes of politics, covetousness, and uncompassionate love. God was not pleased with the relationship she had with the world. I too was upset with her unspiritual condition.

This apostate church was like the five foolish virgins that Jesus described that were not ready for the marriage to the bridegroom. The five wise virgins were ready and went into the marriage but the five foolish ones missed the coming of the bridegroom and the door was shut. They knocked at the door to enter and said, *"Lord, Lord, open to us,"* but the Lord said *"I know you not."* Like it was mentioned to the church at Thyatira, the apostate church as a whole missed the translation to heaven and had to endure the Great Tribulation.

MYSTERY BABYLON

She was filled with an unholy laughter and you could see that written all over her face were words of corruption and violence. She was associated with all of the horrible ungodly nations of the past since the nation of Babylon in the book of Genesis. Those who were proud of her and longed for her sinful leadership called her *"Mystery, Babylon the great."* She was the mother of prostituted spiritual idolatry and linked with the filth, wicked lewdness, and ruthless abominations of the earth. It was painful to watch.

I saw what appeared to be blood all over her. I sensed in an instant that she was drunk with the blood of God's people who were martyrs in the church for many hundreds of years of the church's existence. I could tell that there were many martyrs who died for their pure faith. She was the one who was responsible for killing so many Christians and Jews that opposed her hatred and debauchery.

Just like John who wrote the book of Revelation, I was horrified and filled with wonder. I was amazed because in my heart I knew that she represented the church that was now in the tribulation.

The church which started out with such purity and innocence was now the subject of vile and horrific sin and had become apostate. She forsook her religious faith. She was demonically influenced to be allied with all of the political empires of the world. I didn't understand what I was seeing. I just didn't totally know the meaning of this woman and the horrible Antichrist that she was in alliance with.

In my vision an angel came near to me and asked me if I wanted an explanation of this woman and the evil world leader that she was associated with and the other leaders that had such influence and power. I said yes. Just as I thought, I was informed that she was the worldly church, and the leaders she was connected with were all representative of the major historical nations of past history. This has been going on since the time when the leaders of the church in past history would coronate the Emperors of the Roman Empire which gave birth to this unholy alliance. They were the basis of all the powers that were in existence today.

This Antichrist who appeared and that she was associated with, was similar to the demonic spirits that inhabited the souls of major Antichrist-type individuals of the past. This Antichrist was depicted as coming from a horrible evil filled and darkened past that no one else had escaped from and he was going to be headed for destruction as well.

WAS, IS NOT, YET IS TO COME

Everyone was amazed at this world leader and the woman. All the people of the earth who knew the Lord, understood that this world leader was against the work of Christ. John called him *"the beast that was, and is not, and yet is."* In other words, the evil spirit that was in him, was in power at one time, was not in power at the time of John's writing of the book of Revelation, but was going to be back in power in the future. His evil spirit was in other Antichrists of the past and was now in him. That time of the future was now! We knew that John himself warned us that *"it is the last time: and as ye have heard that Antichrist shall come, even now are there many Antichrists; whereby we know that it is the last time."*

This Antichrist that the woman was associated with had seven heads. He was reminiscent of the evil empires in the past, namely Egypt, Assyria, Babylon, Medo-Persia, Greece, Rome and the Holy Roman Empire representing the seven heads. In the Apostle John's day, five of these empires were in past history, one was in existence, and one was yet to come, and indeed it did come after the time of John the Apostle.

The Antichrist was empowered from those seven kingdoms of the past and was considered the eighth. He had ten horns which were illustrative of the ten kings that were reigning in power with him during the Great Tribulation. He was headed for destruction. The ten nations that he was the leader of came into power with him. They are the ones who give this powerful leader all of his strength and control. As the scripture says, *"These are of one mind, and they will give their power and authority to the beast."*

WAR WITH CHRIST

All of a sudden I saw my third view of Armageddon as the nation's turned on Christ. Christ was returning at the end of the Great Tribulation to fight this battle. His return was far different than when he rode in meekness and humility into Jerusalem with crowds cheering when He was alive on the earth. This time He was coming with power and authority to destroy the enemies of God. He was coming in victory.

Would He be coming back for me? I was there with Him in heaven just before all of these events were happening in the world and I remember how beautiful and peaceful it was. I missed that. I was wondering if Christ would remember who I was and if He knew that it was His Father who sent me back to the earth.

With that picture of Armageddon in my mind, I was amazed and stunned that the Antichrist and his leaders that were with him, turned to fight Christ who was returning in victory. They stopped fighting with the many other nations that had gathered together over the life or death of the nation of Israel and started lobbing their weapons toward the returning Christ. I couldn't believe it. It was all to no avail as Christ totally overwhelmed them. He destroyed them all.

I saw in this vision that Jesus Christ triumphed over them and conquered them to the last man that was standing. He was the King of kings and Lord of lords. Coming back with Him to the earth were all of the Old Testament saints along with the New Testament church that had been translated and had been with Him in heaven. All of these saints of God were the ones who were the chosen ones who were faithful and true to the Lord. Were my wife and children among that number? They had to be! I was there in heaven with them before my return to earth and I so desperately wanted to see them.

Then I saw what appeared to be like a large sea of people that I recognized as representing all of the nations and languages of the world. The leaders of the ten nations that supported the Antichrist had turned on the woman that was associated with him before this great battle began. They no longer supported her power and authority. They stripped her of her ability to have anything to do with the people of the world as they killed many of the leaders of this prostitute church. It was what she deserved as they basically neutralized her and totally took away her power to communicate with those who were previously under her influence. She had no relationship with the Lord and now she lost her relationship with these powerful nations.

A Look Beyond

I began to understand that it was God's will and His plan for the end to come to all the worldly kingdoms of the world, and the beginning of the Kingdom of God on earth. The ten leaders of the ten kingdoms who totally supported the Antichrist were coming to an end. These leaders completely destroyed the influence of the prostitute church who had a powerful influence over all the peoples of the world both spiritually and politically.

The prophetic words of God needed to be fulfilled that were prophesied long ago about the wrath of the Lord our God on earth. I began to realize that God had allowed the destruction of the powerful influence of the Babylonian system that was represented by many of the great nations of the world. The evil nations of the world were Mystery, Babylon. It is described as a city, a series of mountains, and many waters, that had tremendous sway over all the earth. Both the powers of religious and political Babylon had now become its own bitter enemy. It became self-destructive as it turned on itself. The political leaders that were in league with the Antichrist hated its religious counterpart, the apostate church and destroyed her.

I was reminded of America and the self-destruction that it had created for itself. The political system cast the religious system of influence off its back. The political system that desperately needed a solid moral compass had rejected the religious system that had a moral influence in the country for hundreds of years. America was in serious trouble. It had been divided. Many of the States had gone their separate ways. The United States Constitution was in shambles. America had forgotten God, who He was, and how much He had provided for her. Besides the states suffering financially, the corporate businesses of America were suffering as well as many of them went bankrupt.

America had reached its end in a series of changes that brought her to its knees just like all of the great powers of past history. America knew God at one time but eventually lost touch with

Him and lived for the world. It had cast off all of the teachings of righteousness and morality that was part of its founding principles. It then completely turned her back on the one who helped give birth to the nation.

So too, Mystery Babylon had reached the stage of self-destruction. What an ignoble end! Christ was returning to earth and the evil entities of the world were beginning to crumble right before everyone's eyes. I thought, how sad this has to be in the eyes of God. He was the one who along with His Son created all things in the beginning of time but He had to bring it to an end the way that He did. He had no choice but to bring about the destruction of the world and re-create all things.

Chapter Eighteen: Fall of Economic Babylon

Then I saw an angel come down from heaven with tremendous authority as if speaking directly for God. His countenance lit up the earth with brilliant light and radiant intensity. He shouted from one end of the earth to the other saying and repeating that Babylon the great has been destroyed. He identified it more specifically by saying that *"Babylon the great is fallen, is fallen, and has become a dwelling place of demons, a prison for every foul spirit, and a cage for every unclean and hated bird! For all the nations have drunk of the wine of the wrath of her fornication, the kings of the earth have committed fornication with her, and the merchants of the earth have become rich through the abundance of her luxury."*

COME OUT OF BABYLON

All of a sudden an instruction was given as the heavens reverberated with the words *"Come out of her, my people, lest you share in her sins, and lest you receive of her plagues."* The call was given for all of the souls of the earth that came under her influence to run away from her as fast as possible and not to be involved in her dastardly deeds of money and power. Mystery Babylon was coming to her end. Apparently, there was still hope for those who were still alive in the Great Tribulation, who had not taken the mark of the Antichrist, and who wanted to get away from her villainous ways. Sadly, many had already been murdered for their belief.

The nations of the world who basked in her financial freedom were now going to be choked and asphyxiated by the corruption that had long been her hallmark. The Babylonian system was in freefall as practically all of the great institutions had come to an end. She thought that she would live forever like royalty but she was consumed by famine, mourning and death. In the end she will be burned with fire because of the judgment of God. The judgment would occur in just one single day and at one single time.

All of the leaders of the world who were associated with Mystery Babylon cried and wailed loudly as they saw her destruction. On television I heard the crying and moaning all around the world as they saw her demise. They cried out, *'Alas, alas, that great city Babylon, that mighty city! For in one hour your judgment has come.'* Both the evil political and religious systems of the world had met their bitter end. The knowledge of their sins had reached heaven. They had lived with great pleasure but now they were filled with sorrow.

Mystery Babylon wasn't a literal city but it was an amalgamation of city upon city, nation upon nation involving both politics and the religion. There was no appearance of righteous living but a marriage of convenience that benefitted both of them. The church in the tribulation had become immoral with the political leaders of the world, and the world used the church only to improve its status among the people. God was disgusted with that arrangement. They both became rich by the wealth and economic power that they both had improved their status with.

The kings and political leaders who lived luxuriously and who took advantage of the immoral relationship with the righteous way the church was supposed to live, started to cry as they stood afar off and could do nothing about it. The merchants of the earth wailed with grief over her, because no one was buying any of her merchandise and goods anymore as the world went financially bankrupt. They wept as they said "All of our financial investments are totally destroyed. The wealth of our financial empire is forever gone. Our treasuries are empty, our budgets are slashed to zero. Our stock markets are in disarray. What do we do?"

In the end, the banks had closed. Their credit arrangement was destroyed. They had to turn people away who were seeking financial help. Major corporations who had financial power and had influenced morality toward wickedness, laid people off and closed their doors. The movie and music industry that had caused people to imitate their evil art had gone silent after no one could show up for productions. Awards were no longer fashionable as everyone's trouble took the main stage of importance. No one could find small convenience stores open. The armies and navies of the world were completely destroyed at the Battle of Armageddon. They were dismayed and troubled that something like this could happen. They quickly came to the understanding that it was all over.

REJOICING IN HEAVEN

It was then that a realization came over me of my thoughts as I seemed to be in heaven. Was I really there or was I still on earth? I wasn't sure. I saw rejoicing as all of the saints of God, the apostles and the prophets who had been martyred, were justified before God for what they had gone through in the past. The vengeance of God brought judgment upon Mystery Babylon. God's people were happy because of God's revenge that he placed on them. There was tension on the earth but rejoicing in heaven.

David E. Siriano

Unbelievably, a powerful angel took a huge boulder about the size of the side of a mountain, and threw it into the oceans. The waters of the oceans began to swell and overflow their banks as floodwaters impacted the shores of countries all over the world. There was no place for nations of the world to hide. This mighty angel said, *"Thus with violence the great city Babylon shall be thrown down, and shall not be found anymore. The sound of harpists, musicians, flutists, and trumpeters shall not be heard in you anymore. No craftsman of any craft shall be found in you anymore, and the sound of a millstone shall not be heard in you anymore. The light of a lamp shall not shine in you anymore, and the voice of bridegroom and bride shall not be heard in you anymore. For your merchants were the great men of the earth, for by your sorcery all the nations were deceived. And in her was found the blood of prophets and saints, and of all who were slain on the earth."*

It was over. The nations of the world were a complete failure. The fall of Babylon was truly the end of all the wars, calamities, struggles, political envy, rivalries, covetousness, boasting, hate, disobedience, accusations, unrestrained behavior, and ungodliness. Mystery Babylon had met her violent end. It was too late for the world to turn back and reclaim what it once had. Now the reign of Christ was to begin.

This massive collapse of the nations was a fulfillment of the prophecy written by the Apostle Paul of what would happen in the last days, *"But know this, that in the last days perilous times will come: For men will be lovers of themselves, lovers of money, boasters, proud, blasphemers, disobedient to parents, unthankful, unholy, unloving, unforgiving, slanderers, without self-control, brutal, despisers of good, traitors, headstrong, haughty, lovers of pleasure rather than lovers of God, having a form of godliness but denying its power. And from such people turn away!"*

A Look Beyond

The world had become so intelligent and powerful that they never understood who God was. They trusted in their own understanding rather than rely on God and His truth and knowledge. As that prophecy goes on to say, *"Ever learning, and never able to come to the knowledge of the truth."*

Chapter Nineteen: Return of the Lord

I heard unbelievable shouting and rejoicing from a throng of people from all over heaven. All the saints of God who were there, were praising God saying *"Alleluia; Salvation, and glory, and honor, and power, unto the Lord our God"*. The praises of God were rebounding throughout heaven. Everyone was ecstatic over the fact that God had won the victory over the prostitute. She had corrupted people's lives with her association with the Antichrist and the leaders of the nations of the earth throughout the centuries.

The time had come for the prostitute's judgment. She was supposed to be a separate and called out people, but she had corrupted herself with these nations and had forsaken her one true love of the one true God. She had also forsaken her calling to come out from among the worldliness of the nations. I thought, "How could the church have arrived at this condition that was so far away from God?"

As a worldly church, she had participated in the martyrdom of the remnant of righteous Christians, and had become anti-Semitic toward the nation of Israel, God's covenant people. Now the end of her condition was total separation from God. No longer was there a need for that kind of church that was caught up in her own glory. It was a time of sorrow because her demise could have been avoided had she been obedient to God. The idea of a simple and individual relationship with her Savior was gone. She was unrepentant and her corruption was too obvious. The smoke of her destruction was seen by all and it was a punishment that was forever.

Over and over again, everyone in Heaven rejoiced as they along with the twenty-four Elders keep saying, *"Alleluia, Amen, Alleluia."* The Elders fell down before the Father on the throne and worshipped Him. Then, in a miraculous way, voices came from the Throne of God, a multitude of voices that sounded like rushing water and powerful thunder, and they were all saying, *"Praise our God, all ye his servants, and ye that fear him, both small and great. Alleluia: for the Lord God omnipotent reigns. Let us be glad and rejoice, and give honor to him: for the marriage of the Lamb is come, and his wife hath made herself ready."*

MARRIAGE OF THE LAMB

All of Heaven was preparing for the greatest event in all of history. The people of God, namely the Old and New Testament true believers were going to be married to Jesus Christ, the Son of God forever! The rejoicing resounded throughout the heavens. There was an exuberance that was seen and heard but difficult to explain in words. Everyone was happy. They knew the difference between a wedding on earth and the wedding that was taking place in heaven.

My thoughts in heaven and of being married to the Son of God, the Creator of the universe was unimaginable! What excitement! What Joy! What rejoicing for Israel and the church! Now the creature was one with the Creator. God the Father, Jesus the Son, and the Holy Ghost were one with the saints of God from all the ages through the marriage of the Son to the Bride. The ones who loved the Creator and lived for Him on earth were never to be

David E. Siriano

separated from Him again. The love of God's creation was in His heart. He had us forever and would never let us go. This seemed to be the fulfillment of God's romance with His creation!

My vision now was of being a part of the saints of God who were being married to Jesus Christ. As I looked at all of the others, they seemed to appear as pure as glass. No spot or wrinkle of sin in their demeanor or personality. Everyone was dressed in the purest of fine garments. They were pure and white and clean throughout. All of us had worked on our wedding garments by the righteous acts that we did while we were alive on earth. The garments were not earthly garments but they were the righteous deeds that we had lived by. That's the only way I could explain it. Every deed done in the name of Christ seemed to be stitched into the fine textured spiritual garments we were wearing as we were married to Christ forever.

The ceremony was centered on the highest praise to the Lord. Promises of the Lamb to the Bride and the Bride to the Lamb needed not to be spoken. They were known in our hearts and felt with feelings that were too difficult and heart-felt to explain. The promises that were a part of the ceremony were the thousands of promises of God that we had known and lived with while we were on earth. We were now completely rejoicing and singing those promises as a part of the ceremony now that we were in heaven. Everyone knew those promises and they sang them with exuberance! Everyone's voice was beautiful; the sound of the heavenly choir could not be explained! You had to be there!

I saw my wife and my family and they were there as part of this all-consuming presence of God that will be with us forever, never to be separated from Him again. I saw my parents, my grandparents, and my four brothers and sisters. Friends, school co-workers, neighbors and church people who knew Christ, were there. All of them had been translated to heaven as I had and we were all basking in the joy of becoming the Bride of

A Look Beyond

Christ. We were being married to the One who saved us from a life of wretchedness and worldliness.

We are now free from the law that easily condemned us, that we *"should be married to another, even to him who is raised from the dead, that we should bring forth fruit unto God."* Our lives have brought forth fruit and we are now finding completeness as the Bride of Christ, married to Him for eternity! What a joy we have!

There seemed to be millions upon millions of the saints of God all over heaven who were being married to Christ. It was as if when I saw one of them I saw them all, and I was one of them. I was as close to the one who was the farthest away from me as I was to the one who was standing right next to me. It was astounding and it was beautiful. We were as one. It was beyond words. There was nothing that could describe it in our earthly language but I knew that it was much more beautiful than the most beloved thing on earth. It was thrilling!

The marriage of the Lamb had come. There was a call throughout the heavens, *"Blessed are they which are called unto the marriage supper of the Lamb. And he said unto me, these are the true sayings of God."* I remember hearing on earth that those who were part of the marriage of the bride to the Lamb and those who were called to the marriage supper as guests, were two different groups of people. But I knew in a moment that they were one and the same.

The declaration was made during the ceremony that those who were called to the marriage supper of the Lamb were given the name of the Lamb as part of the Bride. They received His name and they bore His title. They were called by His name, "The Bride of Christ." I thought of the promise that was made to the Church of Pergamum during John's day in the book of Revelation, *"To him that overcomes will I give...him a white stone, and in the stone a new name written, which no man knows saving he that receives it."*

The marriage supper when we were married to Christ was not physical food as we had on the earth. Rather, it was a spiritual food that was far beyond the delight of the satisfaction of filling our worldly stomachs we once had. We were feasting on the delight of knowing God the Father and His Son. It was like totally understanding the communion of his body and blood. We too were enjoying what the Apostle Paul called a "Spiritual Body."

Then I was told, *"worship God: for the testimony of Jesus is the spirit of prophecy."* I knew in a moment that the life and teachings of Jesus on earth and a clear witness by His followers who were now in heaven, were the heart of Divine utterance and inspiration. Speaking about Jesus connected you to the essence of the prophetic understanding of His life, ministry, and future rulership as King of Kings and Lord of Lords. We were feasting on knowing God, but perceiving who He was in eternity would be inexhaustible. It would last forever. The unexplainable beauty of our relationship was that we knew every one of God's characteristics, yet learning about Him and who He was would never end. It was clear to me that we understood everything about God, but still we would learn about Him for eternity! I can't explain it any other way. It was unbelievably being fulfilled.

SECOND COMING OF CHRIST

News that we were all returning to earth traveled fast throughout heaven. Everyone who was part of the body of Christ was getting prepared. We were all rejoicing with excitement and joy. The glow on the faces of the angels was easy to see. The buildup of the return to earth was felt by everyone. The armies of heaven were lined up. The time to return was now.

A Look Beyond

Then with sudden revelation, the heavens were split open and we went along with the appearance of Jesus Christ in His Second Coming to the earth. The appearance of His return to earth was strong and powerful. He returned in swiftness as one who was riding on a white horse expressing his pureness as He wore down all opposition to His appearing. We were all going with Him as He returned to the earth.

We as believers had been married to Christ after we went to heaven. We were all wearing our pure wedding garments that we were married in that were white and clean. We were now returning with Him. I saw my wife and my children that were right next to me and I saw other family and friends returning with us too. The Old Testament Patriarchs were there as well as the Godly Prophets and Kings to lead in this great return to earth.

The Apostles of the New Testament were also in the forefront as the heavens were opened for this great climatic event. All of the souls that had been resurrected before the tribulation were there too. Then the world *"...will see the Son of Man coming on the clouds of heaven with power and great glory. And He will send His angels with a great sound of a trumpet, and they will gather together His elect from the four winds, from one end of heaven to the other."*

The white horse of Christ was emblematic of His Royalty, Judgment and War. He is Faithful and True showing that He cannot disappoint. Righteously He judges and makes war indicating that He is right in punishing the enemies of God.

I saw His eyes and they were like a flame of fire and I knew that He could see and judge things correctly. The crowns that were on His head that showed His Kingship were many, and they seemed to enfold each other as if forming as one. His name was written that seemed to engulf His personality that no one else

164

knew. There seemed to be something different about that name because it revealed a different side of His unknowable wonders.

His clothing was bright red as if they were dipped in blood. Everyone knew that it was He that died on the cross for the sins of the world. All the world deeply sensed that it was He that was *"wounded in the house of my friends."* It was the Jewish people completed in Christ who were in a state of joyful sorrow as they looked upon Him *"whom they have pierced."* They realized what their forefathers had done and they began to weep with great bitterness, but yet with a happiness as if one were seeing their own children after a long absence. They were now grateful that they were with Him.

The countenance and personality of Christ was so bright and powerful that these attributes seemed to scream His name. He was returning as the Word of God which was the very expression and revelation of His Heavenly Father.

His words were strong and powerful like a sword as they destroyed the nations of the world. He appeared to the world in order to rule over them with a will that is strong as iron, revealing the power of His wrath that brings about the destruction of the nations. It's as if His feet are stomping grapes of the wrath of Almighty God. This helps Him win the Battle of Armageddon.

His garments display the Name that only He could possess, *"KING OF KINGS, AND LORD OF LORDS."* It tells of His majesty and dominion in His coming Millennial Reign over the earth. All who believed in Him and lived for Him were pleased beyond understanding.

ARMAGEDDON

Then for the last time, I again saw the terror and wrath of the battle of all battles, Armageddon! Apparently God wanted me to see how horrific it was as I saw all of its terrifying details in repeated detail. Birds all over the heavens were swooping in to eat of the flesh of all of those who were killed. The leaders of the world, the armies, the men under their command, and anything that was alive and now dead were being eaten by the birds of prey. It was an awful sight. Hundreds of thousands, and millions were dead. They had attempted to fight against Jesus Christ who had just returned to the earth. They fought not only against Jesus the Son of God, but also tried to fight all of the believers that had followed Him to earth. Everyone was destroyed by Jesus through the power of His words that He spoke!

The Old Testament and New Testament believers representing the church returned with Christ as He fought against the nations of the world. It was Christ and the church against the state, and the church won! The believers who were part of the tribulation church that was meeting in underground places, came out in the open as they saw the returning Christ. The Antichrist and the prophet who had prophesied in the name of the Antichrist were destroyed. They had deceived the people of the world with their marking system. They had received the worship of the people of the world. They were thrown into a lake of fire. I saw the lake of fire from high above the heavens and earth that looked like a multitude of fiery waters that were far outside the Kingdom of God. These fires were burning red hot as far as the eye could see.

Chapter Twenty: 1,000 Years

Then I saw a powerful angel holding chains. He took the Devil and wrapped the chains all around him. I don't know why the Devil couldn't break free of those chains but he couldn't. This angel must have had unusual power from God. He took the Devil that had deceived the nations and threw him into a pit that seemed to have no bottom. It was dark and gloomy with no way out. I knew that this was the time when the nations were going to be free from his deception for 1,000 years while Christ was reigning on the earth. He was going to be bound there *"so that he should deceive the nations no more till the thousand years were finished."*

MILLENNIUM

It is at the beginning of this 1,000 year time, otherwise known as the Millennium, when I saw the Kingdom of Christ at rest and I understood the scripture that said, *"The wolf also shall dwell with the lamb, the leopard shall lie down with the young goat, the calf and the young lion and the fatling together; and a little child shall lead them. The cow and the bear shall graze; their young ones shall lie down together; and the lion shall eat straw like the ox. The nursing child shall play by the cobra's hole, and the weaned child shall put his hand in the viper's den."* Then was brought to pass the intriguing prophecy that said, *"They shall not hurt nor destroy in all my holy mountain."*

This is a time when Christ began to rule with a "rod of iron," and He judged the nations of the world. I seemed to be standing far away but I knew what was happening. I heard the roll call of nations as He separated those that were on His right hand from those who were on His left hand. On Christ's right hand were the sheep or good nations and on His left hand were the goat or evil nations. I heard Him bless the nations on His right hand and tell them, *"Come, ye blessed of my Father, inherit the kingdom prepared for you from the foundation of the world: For I was hungry, and ye gave me meat: I was thirsty, and ye gave me drink: I was a stranger, and ye took me in: Naked, and ye clothed me: I was sick, and ye visited me: I was in prison, and ye came unto me."* They were words of comfort as those nations rejoiced.

I heard the words of Christ as He turned to the nations on His left hand and said, *"Depart from me, ye cursed, into everlasting fire, prepared for the devil and his angels: For I was hungry, and ye gave me no meat: I was thirsty, and ye gave me no drink: I was a stranger, and ye took me not in: naked, and ye clothed me not: sick, and in prison, and ye visited me not."* Those nations were filled with sorrow. Their national names were never to be remembered and were not going to be a part of Christ's coming Kingdom.

The nations who were on Christ's right hand and were blessed by Him were the national names that entered the Millennium. The people of those nations were the ones who helped the poor and fed them, who gave shelter to the homeless, and who visited those in prison. They helped to rule during that time. The nations who were on Christ's left hand and cursed by Him, were nations whose names were lost forever and did not enter the Millennium. The people of those nations did nothing to help those who were in need.

I recalled my Sunday school teachers and Pastors referring to this beautiful one thousand year time here on earth as well. While there was always much argument over the timing of the Lord's return I always believed that the Lord would return before the Millennium and set up those wonderful events. We were now ready to enter into the joy of the Lord. As the scripture says, *"No more shall every man teach his neighbor, and every man his brother, saying, 'Know the LORD,' FOR THEY ALL SHALL KNOW ME, FROM THE LEAST OF THEM TO THE GREATEST OF THEM, SAYS THE LORD. FOR I WILL FORGIVE THEIR INIQUITY, AND THEIR SIN I WILL REMEMBER NO MORE. "* Thank God!

ISRAEL AND THE CHURCH

While I was reminiscing on those thoughts, I saw two classes of people that were going to have authority on the earth while Christ was going to rule. First, there were those who had been translated and had missed the tribulation days. These were the Old Testament believers of Israel and other nations who had followed God's instructions to obey His commandments. Included in that group were the New Testament believers who had repented and believed in Jesus Christ as their Savior during the church age.

They were all sitting on thrones and they were commissioned to judge those who were part of the Millennium, as it says *"I saw thrones, and they that sat upon them, and judgment was given unto them. "* That is in fulfillment of the promise made to the church, *"Do you not know that the saints will judge the world? And if the world will be judged by you, are you unworthy to judge the smallest matters? Do you not know that we shall judge angels? How much more, things that pertain to this life?"* The righteous church was indeed a part of this marvelous time of Christ's reign on the earth.

The second group I saw were those who had to live through the Tribulation. These lives were the ones who had refused to worship the Antichrist or his image and had not taken his mark who were both Jews and Gentiles. They had given their lives as martyrs. They reigned with Christ for the entire Millennium. It says this clearly about the tribulation overcomers, *"Then I saw the souls of those who had been beheaded for their witness to Jesus and for the word of God, who had not worshiped the beast or his image, and had not received his mark on their foreheads or on their hands. And they lived and reigned with Christ for a thousand years. Blessed and holy is he that hath part in the first resurrection: on such the second death hath no power, but they shall be priests of God and of Christ, and shall reign with him a thousand years."*

This time of great rulership and leadership of the nation of Israel during the Millennium was being fulfilled for as it says in the Old Testament, *"And it shall come to pass in the last days, that the mountain of the LORD's house shall be established in the top of the mountains, and shall be exalted above the hills; and all nations shall flow unto it. And many people shall go and say, Come ye, and let us go up to the mountain of the LORD, to the house of the God of Jacob; and he will teach us of his ways, and we will walk in his paths: for out of Zion shall go forth the law, and the word of the LORD from Jerusalem. And he shall judge among the nations, and shall rebuke many people: and they shall beat their swords into plowshares, and their spears into pruning hooks: nation shall not lift up sword against nation, neither shall they learn war anymore."*

Israel became a glorious place during the time of the Millennium for the scriptures say, *"The wilderness and the solitary place shall be glad for them; and the desert shall rejoice, and blossom as the rose. "It shall blossom abundantly, and rejoice even with joy and singing: the glory of Lebanon shall be given unto it, the Excellency of Carmel and Sharon, they shall see the glory of the LORD, AND THE EXCELLENCY OF OUR GOD. "*

Even though the time of the Millennium was for 1,000 years, the time seemed to fly by. The righteous nations of the earth were enjoying themselves during this time, and I was at great peace with my family as I felt the protection of Christ as He ruled successfully. I was living the wonderful promise of long life during this time. It was revealed to me that, *"Never again will there be in it an infant who lives but a few days, or an old man who does not live out his years; the one who dies at a hundred will be thought a mere child; the one who fails to reach a hundred will be considered accursed. "*

All of the nations were learning to get along with one another. There was peace throughout the land. *"He shall judge between many peoples, and rebuke strong nations afar off; they shall beat their swords into plowshares, and their spears into pruning hooks; Nation shall not lift up sword against nation, neither shall they learn war anymore. "*

THE DEVIL LOOSED

Then, the unthinkable happened. The Devil who had been bound for the 1,000 years while Christ and the believers were ruling and reigning, was loosed at the end of that time. I could hardly believe it. He was causing trouble again as he went around to the leaders of the nations to fight again against the God of the whole earth. The Devil gathered them together to once more launch an attack in a final last-ditch effort to overthrow God. Because Christ ruled with a rod of iron during the Millennium and rebellion was limited, this was God's final test for the people of the world to discover whether their allegiance was to Him or to the Devil.

The Devil and the armies surrounded the people of God in the Middle East, and particularly the city of Jerusalem. It was an innumerable army that was with him but he was soundly defeated by fire that came out of heaven from the Throne Room of God that destroyed him and all of the rebellious armies. Once again and for the final time, the nations were stripped and narrowed down to the ones that were truly going to submit to God and His righteousness.

The Devil was then taken from the earth and cast into the same lake of fire that the Antichrist and his prophet were cast into. The Devil and his angels were forever separated from God and the people of God, never to be heard from again. The heavens rejoiced!

WHITE THRONE JUDGMENT

I then saw a Great White Throne that was high above the heavens. It was white because it was filled with the purity of God for everyone to see. The holiness and righteousness of God was now ready to be revealed in His judgments. It was the end of heaven and earth as we once knew it as it disappeared in His regal presence. It was as if we were in a state of suspension and transition as heaven and earth were gone and only His Throne was able to be seen. His presence in the midst of His creation was awesome. Christians were there to observe this remarkable scene though we weren't being judged.

God had already judged the Christians for their works in heaven while the tribulation was happening on the earth. He also had judged the Jewish nation on earth during that tribulation as they faced the persecution by the Antichrist. He had already judged the other nations of the earth that were on His right hand and left hand at the end of the tribulation.

He was now ready to judge those individuals who had not repented and did not believe and trust in Him. They had their opportunity to believe on him during their lifetime on earth but they did not heed His voice or His calling. As the Bible says, *"For since the creation of the world His invisible attributes are clearly seen, being understood by the things that are made, even His eternal power and Godhead, so that they are without excuse, because, although they knew God, they did not glorify Him as God, nor were thankful, but became futile in their thoughts, and their foolish hearts were darkened."*

We saw all of the books that the angels kept as records that were now opened. And lastly, the Book of Life was opened. The people were judged according to what the angels had recorded. Everyone came up in front of the Great White Throne. Everyone who had been buried at sea, everyone who had died and were now in hell came before God and His mighty throne. Everyone was judged. All of death and all of hell were thrown into the lake of fire where the Devil, the Antichrist, and the false prophet were. As the Bible states, *"And as it is appointed unto men once to die, but after this the judgment."*

All the individuals whose names were not found in the Book of Life were thrown into the lake of fire. This lake was like fiery waters to swim in as far as the eye could see. It was larger than the biggest fiery heavenly body in the universe. I saw what appeared like a gigantic sun that was thousands of light years across. No one could see or find the end of it. No one was able to escape it. This was the end, the second death. All of the enemies of God were dealt with and finally as the scripture says, *"The last enemy that shall be destroyed is death."* The

A Look Beyond

Lord God had finally taken control of His creation as I, and all the people of heaven were relieved.

Chapter Twenty-One: New Heaven and New Earth

THE NEW JERUSALEM

Heaven and earth were gone. Now it was time for God to make a New Heaven and a New Earth. We weren't there when God made the original heaven and earth but we saw this creation. It was spectacular as He recreated everything new. There were no more ocean waters as God was now the source and origination of all life. With no ocean, I could only imagine that there were no aquatic animals.

Then I saw the most beautiful sight that I had ever seen. It was the New Jerusalem that was coming down from God out of heaven. It was a city yet it did not look entirely as a city. I realized that it looked more like a Bride that was framed in equality that was eternal in her existence. It was as if she was made of elements that could not be explained. She was like the purest of gems with streets as the brightness of Gold. The city was so filled with the glory of God that it seemed to shine as pure gold and clear as glass. It brightened the universe as it descended to earth. This city, whose length, and breadth, and height were all equal, was the vast body of believers that had been touched by God and changed by His redemptive plan.

A Look Beyond

It was God who was dwelling with His people. He was going to live with them eternally. It was so unusual and so difficult to explain but easy to experience and understand. This vast city was now His people. The New Jerusalem was us! It was never about the buildings or the location. It was not about genetics or the physical, as the mansions were about us dwelling with God.

It was not about how I dressed or what I looked like, it was about us and God! God was with us and He was our Eternal and Ever-existent Life. Forever and ever He was to be with all of us. Then it was burned in my mind the scripture that said *"And God shall wipe away all tears from their eyes; and there shall be no more death, neither sorrow, nor crying, neither shall there be any more pain: for the former things are passed away."*

Then God said *"I am Alpha and Omega, the beginning and the end. I will give unto him that is thirsty of the fountain of the water of life freely. He that overcomes shall inherit all things; and I will be his God, and he shall be my son."* Everyone who was in Heaven felt the separation between those of us who were overcomers from those who were not overcomers and did not make it to heaven. Those of us who were in heaven had lived righteously on earth while we were alive, and those who did not make it to heaven did not live righteously while on earth. Those who were unrepentant of their fear, unbelief, defilement, murders, prostitution, wizardry, idolatry, or who lied, were thrown into the Lake of Fire which is the second death.

We who were the Bride of Christ were now the eternal wife of the Son, the Lamb of God. We were the ones who were also seen by John and described as the New Jerusalem. We now were and will always be the Holy City of Jerusalem that came from God. It was as if we were an integral part of the framework of the city yet alive as individuals within the city. God was now in us and we were in Him. We as the City of God now had the glory of God in and through us. It was an unbelievable experience. You

176

would have to be alive and in the city to understand it. There are no other words to explain it.

The glory of God shining in us as a city depicted God's Glory in every part of the gates and in the foundation to the city. They appeared to be made with physical stones but in reality, the gates and the foundation seemed to have a life of their own, crystal clear and most precious.

THE GATES AND FOUNDATION

The gates to the city had an angel posted at each one of them. There were twelve gates that glistened like Pearl stones and each of them had the names of the twelve Tribes of Israel inscribed on them. The Spirit of God gave me a reminder of what the tribal names stood for at the city's gates. Every one of us entering the city had a spiritual knowledge that the primary beginning of all that we have with God came through His first relationship with a family that became the nation of Israel. They were the first family and nation who were called to serve God and be committed to a right relationship with Him.

God's promise to Abraham and then given to Jacob was that *"in thee shall all families of the earth be blessed."* Without the nation of Israel there would be no other families of the earth that God could bless. Without the nation of Israel there would be no church for Him to live through. Without the nation of Israel there would be no heaven that we could enjoy!

The covenant that God had with Israel was the beginning of the relationship that God had with all of the people of the earth who would serve Him. It was no longer just one nation or group of people, it was God who was offering salvation to the entire world through Jesus Christ. This pathway through Israel to God was for all people to come to believe who He was and what He could do for them. These gates were symbols of our entrance to know God and the pathway to His presence. As believers, we were now a part of the doorway that Israel opened to our spiritual success. Being a part of this holy city was based on this knowledge and understanding.

The foundations of the city were engraved with the names of the twelve Apostles. Each of the layers of the foundation were shining with all manners of precious stones. And just as the twelve Tribes of Israel were the doorway to the city, so the twelve Apostles were the foundation and strength of truth and doctrine for the new city. They were the beginning spirit that was needed for the church to be an integral part of His salvation for the world. As we looked at the foundation, we could see ourselves glistening in them because of their labor and work of love. The entire city was built upon their initial relationship as disciples who followed Christ. Their life teachings and principles became the basis upon which the entire city was built upon. We were there because of their knowledge and understanding of the early principles of Christ.

The spirit and intent of the apostles and prophets leadership was known and felt. I was reminded of the scripture which said *"Now therefore ye are no more strangers and foreigners, but fellow citizens with the saints, and of the household of God; And are built upon the foundation of the apostles and prophets, Jesus Christ himself being the chief corner* stone; *In whom all the building fitly framed together grows unto an holy temple in the Lord."*

The most amazing beauty of the city was the fact that there was no need of a church, nor synagogue, nor a temple because God the Father and the Lamb were the focus of worship for the entire city. The Father and the Lamb were the Temple of praise and worship for all the people of heaven. We were able to understand, enter into, and be a part of all of the attributes of God. He was alive in us with all of His love. It was like He was in us and we were in Him. The brilliance of worship unto Him was known and felt throughout the city. It was the same thing for the lighting of the city. There was no need of the sun or the moon because God and the Lamb were the light of everything and everyone in the city. There was no sunset and no dawn because the light was a forever light.

The nations of the earth who had been saved and were judged as righteous, were all affected by the light of this great city. The light of God and His son shined on these nations. The kings of those nations gave honor to that great city. They gave glory and honor unto the Lord and to the inhabitants of that city. The gates are to be continually open all day as there will be no night there. Only the righteous were free to enter in and out of the city and were able to move freely everywhere. Only those whose names were written in the Lamb's Book of Life were in the New Heaven and New Earth and in the New Jerusalem. These were the redeemed and they were separated, far from those who were defiled and who were in the Lake of Fire.

It was truly then that I understood the scripture that said, *"that He would grant you, according to the riches of His glory, to be strengthened with might through His Spirit in the inner man, that Christ may dwell in your hearts through faith; that you, being rooted and grounded in love, may be able to comprehend with all the saints what is the width and length and depth and height – to know the love of Christ which passes knowledge; that you may be filled with all the fullness of God."*

Chapter Twenty-Two: The River and Tree of Life

Then at last, I saw the River of the Water of Life and the Tree of Life as they both came from the Throne of God and from the Lamb of God, Jesus Christ. I could see the beauty of the Tree of Life as it surrounded the River of Water of Life. The Tree of Life was in the middle of the street of gold and on either side of the River of Life. In other words it was everywhere.

The river and the tree were there to show the power of God and the Lamb to give eternal life to all who believed in them and who now lived with them. The leaves of the tree were there because they healed the nations and the people of the nations. The water of life was for drinking eternally in the presence of God. Both the river and tree were there for the spiritual pleasure and growth for all of God's people. With the Devil being destroyed in the Lake of Fire there was no fear to eat from the tree of life. The water and tree were there for the people and nations with the purpose of giving life to all.

The curse from the Garden of Eden was gone. That curse because Adam and Eve ate from the tree of the knowledge of good and evil was no more. The ban from eating of the tree of life was non-existent. The Throne of God and of the Lamb of God were now the center of attention in the New Heaven and New Earth.

Everyone was able to see the face of God and all who saw Him shall serve Him and bear His mark in their foreheads. His mark was as if we were mirroring the glory of God as it reflected on our faces. It was a beauty to behold as each of us looked at each other with love and assurance.

With the curse being gone, we were never to be deceived by the Devil again. No spirit of darkness would come from him so there was no night that was there. Every moment was as bright as the previous moment. There was no need of the sun to brighten us. No one needed any other light than what was portrayed in the Glory of God and the Lamb.

I, my family and my friends were all a part of the New Heaven and the New Earth! For all of eternity we will be worship, sing, and discover our inexhaustible Savior and God. We will be in a place of fellowship, service, and rulership.

What I had seen of all the glories of heaven meant that my entire previous concepts about life and reality on earth were instantly and dramatically changed once I was in heaven. The throne, the crowns, the twenty-four Elders and the four living Creatures were all a part of my heavenly reality. I was seeing things with my spiritual understanding and not my physical eyes. In heaven I was seeing things with my spirit and not with my earthly senses. I saw things but they were not with my earthly eyes. I heard things but they were not with my earthly ears. My thought processes were not with my earthly mind.

God and His reality made every concept on earth a non-entity. My heavenly reality was no longer my earthly reality. I now looked at things in heaven with God's knowledge and not man's knowledge. Everything had changed. What I could not grasp on earth I was now comprehending in heaven.

It was then that I understood the scripture that said, *"For my thoughts are not your thoughts, neither are your ways my ways, saith the LORD. For as the heavens are higher than the earth, so are my ways higher than your ways, and my thoughts than your thoughts."*

BACK TO REALITY

Suddenly, I heard a sharp noise. I shook myself and opened my eyes. I was in bed. The alarm clock was ringing. I was awakened from what seemed to be a deep sleep. For a moment I didn't know where I was but an amazing feeling of satisfaction came over me. The sun was shining through the windows and I heard the voices of my wife and three children readying for the day filling the atmosphere. It felt like I was no longer in heaven but I was back on earth. I was with my family. I felt like I was shaking, but a great relief and excitement came over me!

What just happened to me? I thought I was part of the translation of the church to heaven and then told by God that I must return to earth and live through the Great Tribulation. I thought I had a realization that I was there with God but now that I was awake from sleep, it appears like I was not. Was it all a dream? Was it a vision? At first I wasn't sure, but I do know one thing, there was an awakening in my spirit! My life would never be the same. I got out of bed and I hugged my wife and children as they came near me and never wanted to let them go. I wept as I saw them. As I woke from my sleep, I appeared to them to be shaken and upset but I tried to explain to them that I had a powerful experience that could not be imagined. They sat there extremely interested as I tried my best to explain to them what had happened to me.

Just trying to understand it myself, I related to them that apparently I had a series of visions. In those visions I was taken to heaven, saw the throne of God, the twenty four Elders, the four living creatures, and I received my rewards. Those visions brought me back to earth to live through the entire Great Tribulation of famine, war, disease and poverty. I saw and talked to some of those who were of the 144,000 servants of God. I felt the horror of the seven angels who had the trumpet judgments and the seven angels who had the wrath of God's judgments. I heard about the 200 million strong army that was the focus of television news. I understood the appearance of the Antichrist and his false prophet.

My family understood and were just happy that I was OK. It seems that I had seen these visions to know what the Apostle John wrote about in the book of Revelation. I was given them so that I could appreciate all that we will have in heaven in the future and to warn those here on earth of the coming calamities that will happen in the Great Tribulation.

Because of the visions that God gave to me, I have a message to everyone I come in contact with, "live for God and His Word and He will never fail you." I'm giving a warning to bring people back to the Biblical teachings of what has happened in the past and what is about to happen in the future. I must do my part in spreading the Gospel of Jesus Christ as the only way of salvation. The prophecies from Genesis to Revelation are now more real to me than ever before. I realize that time is short and an eternity without God is waiting for those who do not believe in Him. The message must go forth. I must be able to convey on earth what is to come. I must tell others about the Master Plan that God has for the nations of the earth. I must tell people about the Second Coming of Christ. My prayer is "Use me Lord, Here am I, send me."

The harvest is ready before Christ returns to earth. Our generation and every generation that follows must tell of His soon coming. We must tell our friends so that they can tell others that the time is short. God needs us to respond to the call that He has on our lives and to tell others about Him. Every generation must feel the burden and obligation to witness to as many as we can as if we were pulling them out of the fires of condemnation and

A Look Beyond

hell. There isn't much time left. We need to obey His word that says, *"Go ye into all the world, and preach the gospel to every creature."* We must want to do our part for every person we come in contact with as the Bible says, *"Let your light so shine before men, that they may see your good works, and glorify your Father which is in heaven."*

The beauty of what God the Father has done is expressed in this scripture that says, *"For God so loved the world, that he gave his only begotten Son, that whosoever believeth in him should not perish, but have everlasting life. For God sent not his Son into the world to condemn the world; but that the world through him might be saved. He that believeth on him is not condemned: but he that believeth not is condemned already, because he hath not believed in the name of the only begotten Son of God."*

I now look at the Book of Revelation with a different mindset. It may be difficult to understand, but it holds the key to the success of righteous living for believers and the demise of those who are disobedient to Christ. As the scripture says, *"...now is the accepted time; behold, now is the day of salvation."*

As we approach the end of time, everyone must hear God's voice that will reverberate in our hearts throughout all of the Earth. As the Book of Revelation says, *"These sayings are faithful and true: and the Lord God of the holy prophets sent his angel to shew unto his servants the things which must shortly be done. Behold, I come quickly: blessed is he that keeps the sayings of the prophecy of this book."*

The call goes out as if to endorse what had already happened in history, *"He that is unjust, let him be unjust still: and he which is filthy, let him be filthy still: and he that is righteous, let him be righteous still: and he that is holy, let him be holy still."*

I remembered what the Apostle John wrote, *"I am Alpha and Omega, the beginning and the end, the first and the last. Blessed are they that do his commandments that they may have right to the tree of life, and may enter in through the gates into the city.*

For without are dogs, and sorcerers, and whoremongers, and murderers, and idolaters, and whosoever loves and making a lie. I Jesus have sent mine angel to testify unto you these things in the churches. I am the root and the offspring of David, and the bright and morning star.

And the Spirit and the bride say, Come. And let him that hears say, Come. And let him that is athirst come. And whosoever will, let him take the water of life freely. For I testify unto every man that hears the words of the prophecy of this book, If any man shall add unto these things, God shall add unto him the plagues that are written in this book:

And if any man shall take away from the words of the book of this prophecy, God shall take away his part out of the book of life, and out of the holy city, and from the things which are written in this book. He which testifies these things says, surely I come quickly. Amen. Even so, come, Lord Jesus."

THE END!
OR IS IT REALLY THE BEGINNING?

About the Author

David Siriano is a graduate of Zion (Northpoint) Bible College in Haverhill, MA with a theological degree in Bible. He served as a Pastor in the New England States and New York for 45 years until 2008. No longer Pastoring, he is now available to travel and conduct End Times prophecy seminars nationwide.

Throughout his ministry, David has had an avid interest in Eschatology, the study of End Time events. He has devoted much of the past 40 years studying and teaching on that subject. As a social eschatologist, he has conducted numerous seminars in the states of New York, Massachusetts, Connecticut, Rhode Island, Vermont, New Hampshire, Pennsylvania, Maryland, Florida and throughout the east coast on the End-Times message of the Bible and how it relates to the news events of today.

He specializes in the Biblical Apocalyptic books of Daniel and Revelation, the Old Testament Tabernacle, and the Major and Minor Prophets. He is a college guest lecturer and teacher at Northpoint Bible College in Haverhill, MA, and at Crossroads Cathedral International Bible Institute in East Hartford, CT.

His other books are:

The Cultural Collapse of America, and the World

Intergalactic Warfare

He and his wife, Elsa May, have been married fifty-three years and reside in West Henrietta, NY. They have two children David and Darla who are involved in Christian ministry: David at The

Church of North Orlando in Florida and Darla at Faith Temple in Rochester, NY. They are blessed with eight grandchildren.

To contact David for speaking engagements, please email desir63@aol.com.

CPSIA information can be obtained
at www.ICGtesting.com
Printed in the USA
FFOW03n1337190417
34573FF